WHEN
JEFF
COMES
HOME

WHEN JEFF COMES HOME

Catherine Atkins

G. P. PUTNAM'S SONS ▐ NEW YORK

G. P. PUTNAM'S SONS
a division of
Penguin Putnam Books for Young Readers,
345 Hudson Street, New York, NY 10014.
G. P. Putnam's Sons, Reg. U.S. Pat. & Tm. Off.
Published simultaneously in Canada.
Printed in the United States of America.
Book designed by Semadar Megged
Text set in Trump Mediaeval

Library of Congress Cataloging-in-Publication Data
Atkins, Catherine.
When Jeff comes home / Catherine Atkins.   p. cm.
Summary: Sixteen-year-old Jeff, returning home after
having been kidnapped and held prisoner for three years,
must face his family, friends, and school and
the widespread assumption that he engaged
in sexual activity with his kidnapper.
ISBN 0-399-23366-0
[1. Kidnapping—Fiction. 2. Child sexual abuse—Fiction.]
I. Title.   PZ7.A862Wh   1999
[Fic]—dc21   98-44016   CIP   AC

5 7 9 10 8 6 4

To my Grandmother

Catherine Tuohy Bass

WHEN
JEFF
COMES
HOME

PRELUDE

Dad never believed me later, when I told him there was nothing he could have done. . . .

"I'm so thirsty," Brian whined, flopping his skinny arms over the front seat of the Jeep and panting like a dog. My stepmother, Connie, peered back at him over her sunglasses, grinning. Dad drove on, hands firm on the wheel. I could see one individual drop of sweat sliding down the back of his neck. Even in April, California's Central Valley was hot and dry. We were fifteen miles outside Fresno, heading back to Wayne after spending most of spring vacation in San Diego.

"I'm not stopping again," Dad said finally. "We just had lunch. We have to make time now. It's almost two o'clock, and Jeff's game is at six. As it is, we won't be home until close to five." Brian slumped down next to me in the second seat. He sighed, folding his arms across his chest.

"Jeff," Dad called back to me, turning his head slightly, "you ready to pitch tonight?" The question was rhetorical. We both knew I was. We had done all the tourist things in San Diego—the zoo, Balboa Park, Sea World, a Padres game—but Dad and I had worked out every morning and he'd also caught for me in the park near our hotel.

"Sure, Dad, no problem," I said, hoping Brian hadn't noticed how much warmer Dad's voice was when he spoke to me. I looked to the back of the Jeep to catch Charlotte's reaction, but only my sister's denim-clad knees were visible. Kneeling up on the seat, I leaned over to talk with her. Charlotte lay on her back, a book propped up against her knees.

"You want something to drink?" I asked quietly. She rolled her eyes in Dad's direction.

"Sure, why not? Dad," she called, "we had lunch two hours ago. I'm with Brian."

Revitalized, Brian sat up. "Yeah! Let's take a vote. Jeff?" He looked at me eagerly, knowing my vote counted for more than his and Charlie's put together.

Of the three of us, Brian was the only one who resembled Dad at all. Same brown eyes, same brown hair, same regular features. He did his best to act like him too, an eight-year-old version of a conservative, opinionated lawyer. Yet Dad was as indifferent to him as he was cold and disapproving to Charlie. Connie did not seem to notice. Her main interest was Dad and she spent most of her energy keeping him happy, though she worked too, as a sixth grade teacher at the elementary school we attended in Wayne. Charlie was in her class this year, while I was in eighth grade, about to graduate over to Wayne High.

Brian waited for my answer, staring at me impatiently.

"Yeah, I could use a drink." I turned to my stepmother. "Connie, how about you?"

Before she could answer, Dad said, "It's up to you. Do we waste a half hour getting off this damn highway and finding some place because the kids are bored, or do we move forward in a disciplined manner?"

Though Dad's tone was serious, I knew he had seen the humor in the situation. I leaned forward, hanging over the seat as Brian had done. Connie paused for effect, her light brown hair swirled high on her head in a ponytail, one finger holding her place in the latest Danielle Steel.

"Drinks," she said finally, holding back a smile. Dad groaned, and we cheered.

"Okay. This has to be quick. I'm not getting off in Fresno, so look for something right off the highway."

We had been passing ugly, blighted-looking fields of yellow weeds for miles, but billboards for businesses in Fresno had started to appear.

" 'Rest area ahead,' " Dad read off one sign. "That's us. We'll pull in, find a vending machine, and leave."

He waited for objections and heard none. I couldn't wait to get out just to stretch my legs.

Tall hedges lined either side of the driveway into the rest stop, curving around in an upside-down U shape that led back to the highway. Dad cruised by a Winnebago, the only other vehicle in sight, and pulled into a shady spot near some picnic tables and a stand of scrub oak trees. The vending machines and bathrooms were a football field's length away across an artificial-looking green lawn bisected by concrete walkways.

"Dad," Charlotte moaned, "can't you park any closer?"

"The walk will do you good," he said briskly.

"Yeah, the walk'll do you good," Brian echoed, turning back to grin at her.

"A walk will do us all good," Connie said, stepping out of the Jeep.

I jumped out and began jogging in place. The air held a yellow haze from the factories around Fresno, and I could smell the carbon monoxide from the thousands of cars passing by on Interstate 5. I took a deep breath anyway, shaking my hands out, then stretching my arms far back over my head.

"You can't wait, can you?" Dad stood next to Connie by the driver's side door, watching me, smiling.

"For the game? Yeah, I wish it was starting now. I feel ready." I was pitching the season opener for my Little League team, the Bobcats, against our division rivals, the Eagles, at Standard Field that night. My best friend, Vin Perini, was catching and I wanted to call him before the game and talk strategy.

Brian tugged at my arm. "Come on, Jeff, race you!"

I laughed. "Wait a minute, let's find out what everyone wants."

"I'll take a Diet Pepsi or Coke, whichever they

have," Connie said, leaning back against Dad. He put his arms around her waist and smiled.

"I'll take anything with caffeine," he said. "Come on, Con, let's check this place out." Dad and Connie walked off together toward the picnic area.

"Okay, Brian," I said, "I'll race you. You get a five-second head start. Go!"

Brian took off like he had been shot out of a cannon. Charlie and I grinned at each other and started counting out loud.

By the time we reached five, Brian was a third of the way to the vending machines. I sprinted after him, my legs eating up the ground. I caught my brother in an instant, stayed even with him, then ran on ahead. I stopped, barely winded, at the entrance to the redwood and concrete enclosure that housed the vending machines.

"You're too fast," Brian puffed, when he pulled up a few seconds later.

I ruffled his hair. "You had me going there for a minute, though," I told him. "What do you want?"

There were two drink machines, one filled with sweetened teas, the other with soft drinks.

"Mountain Dew!" he exclaimed, dropping four quarters in the machine and punching the button. The chilled can plunked down and Brian grabbed it, holding it against his forehead.

"Charlie will want one too," I said, dropping four more quarters in for her drink.

"She shouldn't have that. It's fattening," he said, so primly I had to laugh. I glanced up. Charlie was taking her time, stopping to read a plaque mounted on a concrete block in the grassy area we had just crossed.

"What's it to you?" I asked Brian, who looked blank. " 'It's fattening'—what the hell are you talking about?"

"That's what Dad said. He told Mom to stop buying Mountain Dew, because Charlie's getting too fat."

"What Charlie wants to drink is her own business. Leave her alone about that, okay?"

Brian looked down. "Sure, Jeff. Sorry."

I touched his hair again. "Don't worry about it. She's got Dad on her back enough. She doesn't need us bugging her, right?" I deliberately threw in "us," thinking that would impress him more.

"Okay, Jeff," he said, smiling up at me.

As Charlie reached us, I asked her casually, "Mountain Dew okay?"

"Yeah, thanks," she smiled. On a ninety-degree day, Charlie was dressed in a baggy purple T-shirt and jeans, the better to hide her body. She thought she was enormous, while I told her "chubby" was stretching it. I didn't give a damn either way. To me she was just Charlie, my sister with the same blond hair, green eyes and full mouth I had.

I got a root beer for myself, then patted my pockets. "That's it, I'm out of change. Brian, do you have any?" He shook his head. "Charlie?"

"No, I spent all my money on magazines in the hotel gift shop this morning."

"Damn," I muttered. "We should have gotten their drinks first. You guys go back and see if Dad or Connie has any change. I'll wait for you."

As Charlie and Brian took off, I popped my drink open and took a swig. The root beer was ice-cold and sweet, and I drank deeply, tilting my neck back.

An arm around my waist, a firm man's body behind mine, the sudden, close odor of tobacco and sweat, my head tilted farther back, cold metal pressed against the pulse point of my neck, the root beer dropped, thudding onto the concrete floor, rolling, its contents gurgling out in a steady flow. I struggled instinctively, thrashing my arms, then froze as I felt the metal advance against my skin.

"Yeah, you have a knife at your throat." The very calmness of the man's voice made it more frightening. "Listen now. Do what I tell you."

I didn't move or speak, but he applied more pressure to the knife. A small noise escaped me as I felt its point enter me, and he laughed softly. I raised my hand slowly back to touch my neck, and felt a tiny amount of sticky blood.

"Walk with me."

When I remained frozen, fingers spread over the tiny wound, he tightened his arm around my waist.

"We can always wait for the kids to come back. But you're the only one I want, so I'd have to kill them."

The man turned me around and marched me out of the redwood gazebo, opposite the way Brian, Charlie and I had come in. Only a short concrete walkway separated us from a side parking lot that was empty except for a late model blue van. The van's side panel was open a crack and I wondered if someone else was inside. More scared of what was coming than the knife now pressed against my bare stomach, I stopped walking. The man banged into me, cursing. Then he laughed.

"Please . . . " I managed to choke, stopping when he laughed again.

"No!" he said mockingly, releasing me briefly and shoving me forward. I tripped on the uneven sidewalk and would have fallen had he not caught me. With one arm still wrapped around my stomach, he slid the van door all the way open. The sound was shockingly loud in the deserted lot. The van's interior was empty except for a pile of blankets and a green plastic garbage bag.

"Get in," he ordered, the sarcasm gone now from his voice. I looked back for my family as the man gave me a final shove into the van and climbed in after me.

I DON'T KNOW HOW LONG WE SAT THERE, AFTER. I thought we might be in Wayne, near the street where I used to live, but I wasn't sure. Ray hadn't had much to say during the trip, and I knew better than to watch the road or ask too many questions.

He took a long drag off his Marlboro, held it, then exhaled a cloud of smoke that mingled with the visible puffs our breaths made in the icy air. The silence was broken only by the patter of rain hitting the car. Suddenly he sighed, then rolled his window down and tossed the cigarette out. Leaving the window open, he clasped the steering wheel with both hands.

"Well?" Ray hadn't talked for a while and his voice was froggy. Clearing his throat, he turned his head and spat out the window. I willed my hands steady on my thighs and chanced a look at him.

"Yes sir?"

Ray faced me, lip curled in a half sneer. I could barely make out his features in the half-light provided by a streetlight a quarter block away. Whoever had put the light in was planning ahead; there was nothing but a field and a half-cleared lot on the asphalted road where we were parked.

"You're here. 'Home.' Now get out."

"I . . ."

"Get out."

I reached for the door handle, but continued to watch Ray. I pushed the handle down and cracked the door an inch. The interior light came on. Moving deliberately, I pushed the door another inch. Rain spattered my hand and wrist.

As I had expected, Ray lunged across the seat for me. I stayed absolutely still, forcing myself not to flinch as he clasped me in an awkward embrace. I closed my eyes and retreated. Time meant nothing. I concentrated on the small sounds—the squeak of my leather jacket as Ray shifted, his quick harsh breaths, my own calm, measured breathing. I only hoped he couldn't feel how fast my heart was pounding.

Ray squeezed me hard, once, and brushed his lips across my hair. "Love you," he whispered. I kept my eyes closed, hands in my lap.

"I love you, Ray," I said. He pushed me back and put his hand under my chin. Opening my eyes, I smiled at him. Ray's face held its familiar mix of need and cruelty. His fingers pinched. "I don't have to go," I told him. "Are you sure you want me to?"

He dropped his hand. "It's what you want, kid. You can stay, I told you that." Ray pushed back his thick black hair. "It's not too late for us to drive away. Hell, we could go anywhere."

I kept smiling. It was impossible to know what Ray wanted me to do, or what he would allow me to do. "Um . . . is this Wayne?"

"Yeah, it's Wayne."

"I didn't think—"

"You didn't think what?"

I glanced out the window. I could see a row of darkened houses across the field to my left. I knew now one of them used to be mine. "I didn't know you knew where my family lived, or . . . I mean, we never talked about it."

Ray snorted. "There was a profile of your family in *Time* magazine, I saw your father on TV a couple times, it wasn't hard to find out." This was news to me, but I was careful to show no reaction. "You saw that poster outside Palm Desert," he added.

I could still recall the shock of seeing my face on the mini-mart window the first time Ray took me out with him. He had sworn and peeled out of the lot. I pretended I hadn't seen anything. But he didn't let me outside again for months.

"That was a long time ago," I said carefully.

"Look, I'm not about to convince you. You want to go, go. You don't, then let's get out of here." The harshness of his words was belied by his steady, measuring gaze. He shook his head slightly and reached out for me again. Quickly he kissed the side of my mouth, then pushed me toward the door. "I think you should go."

Outside, I looked back into the car. The rain darkened the windows and the streetlight threw odd shadows on the glass. I couldn't make out Ray's face. I raised my hand in a half wave, then started walking, using the streetlight as my guide. My legs were cramped from sitting so long, and I moved awkwardly, consciously keeping a slow pace so he wouldn't feel I was running from him. I resisted the temptation to look back.

The rain plastered my hair to my forehead and cheeks in long tangles and I realized how cold and uncomfortable I was. I unzipped my jacket and checked the inside pocket. The Dodgers' cap Ray had pressed upon me was still there. I pushed my hair back and put the cap on. As I hesitated, I heard Ray put the car in motion. I began walking again, not hurrying, and soon I saw the sign. I remembered what was on it before I was close enough to read it: Sunnyvue Avenue—the road I'd just come from, and Woodglen Drive—my old street. Ray trailed me, about a hundred yards behind, headlights off. I turned the corner and took a deep breath. My house, the white house where I had lived for three years before Ray took me, stood just beyond the grassy vacant lot where my brother and sister and I had played football and Frisbee. I walked through the lot, ignoring the sopping wet weeds that pulled at my jeans. Moving closer, I saw the house numbers, 3064, gleaming in polished brass. I had put those numbers up myself, under Dad's direction, the summer I turned thirteen.

I walked across the lawn, stopping when I reached the walkway. I couldn't imagine walking up those four steps to the porch. What then? Walk in? Knock? And say what? What if Ray followed me inside? Briefly I considered the unimaginable picture of my dad and Ray in the same room.

Ray tapped his horn lightly, so lightly I could barely hear it, but I jumped. He flicked the lights at me three times. I backed a step toward the house, but couldn't force myself any farther. After a moment, I heard a car door slam.

"Oh God, no," I whispered, "no, no, Ray." I walked back across the lawn to head him off, plastering a smile to my face. But Ray merely stood next to his car, arms folded.

"This is your house, isn't it?" he hissed. I nodded. "Then go in! What the hell do you think you're doing?"

"I will, Ray, I am," I told him, backing up all the way to the porch steps. After another hard look at me, Ray retreated into the Lexus and pulled the car forward, out of sight. I watched him go, my heart thudding against my chest.

The door burst open behind me and I heard a man shout, "Hands up, now!" I turned to face him, hands at my side. Squinting into the porch light, I slowly removed my cap.

A tall man in sweat pants and a T-shirt stood rigid on the top step, arms trembling in the firing position. I could make out the steel gleam of a revolver in the muted yellow light. A woman stood behind him in the door, another taller woman behind her with a boy.

Slowly the man lowered his arms. He stared at me, coming down a step.

"Who are you?" His voice shook. "Do you have something to do with Jeff Hart?" He sounded angry. Then, much more tentatively, "Are you Jeff?"

For a moment I wanted to say, "Not exactly." Instead, I nodded. One of the women cried out, but I did not look away from my father. He came down to me and I noted dully that Dad and I were the same height now. He looked at me for a long moment, then groaned, a harsh, animal cry that made me retreat.

Dad wrapped his arms around me in a tight embrace. Repeating my name, he began to sob, his body convulsing against mine, his tears hot against my cheek. I held myself stiffly, fiercely embarrassed and uncomfortable. My stepmother Connie, sister Charlotte and brother Brian watched from the doorway, Connie's arms around the kids.

It was what I had dreamed of ever since I'd been taken. Yet I felt nothing. Or rather, nothing like I'd imagined. I was cold, and ashamed, terrified that Ray would come back at any moment. I wanted Dad to let me go, but I knew the moment he did the questions would start.

The air shifted and the rain began coming down with more force. Dad released me reluctantly.

"Come on, let's go in," he said, placing his hands on my shoulders and gently pushing me up the stairs. Charlotte, Connie and Brian retreated into the house ahead of us as I moved forward like a zombie.

A siren sounded somewhere in the distance.

"Damn. The police," Dad said, ushering me inside and shutting the door firmly behind him. "Connie?"

"I'll deal with them. What should I say?"

Dad rubbed his face, then stared at the gun in his hand as though he did not recognize it. "I don't know. Anything. But not tonight. I don't want them in here tonight."

"Why are the police coming?" I asked, trying to sound casual. Had they seen Ray outside talking to me? No one answered.

The house was an explosion of warmth and light. Too much. I recoiled from the overheated air and from the four strangers staring at me. Clammy sweat broke out across my forehead, mixing with the rainwater that dripped from my hair.

"Jeff, is it really you?" Connie said suddenly. "Can I . . . ?" She reached out tentatively and pushed my hair back. I tolerated her touch, weaving a little as she threw me off balance. "Of course it is," she murmured. "I see it now. Your eyes, your face. Oh, Kenny, look at him."

"I see him," Dad said, then cleared his throat. I glanced over at him. He tried to smile, a peculiar grimace that twisted his face. Then he turned away, hiding his face in his hands, and we were all silent.

The noise of the siren had been unbearable as it approached, but the sharp, sudden cutoff was worse. I saw the reflection of the flashing red light through the living room blinds and I knew I was trapped.

"Please, I don't want to talk to them." My voice broke and I began to shiver. "I can't. Not now."

"You don't have to," Dad said, coming over to me. "Not now."

"I'll handle it," Connie said, going out to meet them.

I didn't know where to look. Dad, eerily repeating Ray's gesture, put his hand under my chin and raised my head to meet his eyes.

"You're all right, aren't you, Jeff? I've been so worried about you, for so long." He looked at me searchingly, then froze. "What is this?" He reached up and touched my ear.

"Oh," I said, stepping back from him, reaching up too late to hide the diamond ear stud Ray had given me. "It's nothing, just . . . " We stared at each other for a moment, then I looked away. "I'm really tired. If I could just lie down for a while . . . "

"How come you have a Dodgers' cap?" Brian asked. I stared down at the cap, still curled up in my hand. I had forgotten all about it.

"Were you in Los Angeles?" Dad sounded angry. "I looked for you there so many times."

I closed my eyes. "Please let me sleep."

He paused. "Sure. Of course. Plenty of time to talk this over later. Go on upstairs. Your room is just the way you left it."

"Thanks. I'm sorry. . . . " He waved off my apology and turned away.

I STARED AT THE CEILING, LYING ON MUSTY sheets under my old blue comforter. Now that I had Dad's permission to sleep, I couldn't do it.

The window facing the street was just a few feet away from my bed. I knew Ray could be out there now, leaning against his car maybe, waiting for me to give it up and come join him.

That's stupid. He doesn't want to be arrested. He's gone.

But I sat up, pushing the covers back, naked, shivering in the winter air.

I did not want to look. I wanted to find Dad and ask him to look for me. I wanted him to tell me that Ray was not outside, and even if he was, he would never let him near me again.

I made it to the window, and, kneeling to hide myself, pulled the curtain to one side.

The porch light was still on. The police car had left, and it was no longer raining. I did not see anyone outside, and I should have turned away then, but I couldn't. Narrowing my eyes to try to see beyond the space illuminated by the light, I leaned forward, searching.

As my eyes adjusted to the dark, I froze, horrified, as I thought I saw the silhouette of a man standing against the far corner of the house. I squinted, hoping the outline would reveal itself as something else: a hedge, some gardening equipment, the shadow of a tree . . . but the image only became more defined. Finally I broke contact, looking down, not wanting to believe my eyes.

You're imagining things, you half want him to be out there, the "bad" part of you wants that. . . .

I looked again, boldly, almost certain I would see nothing. But the man had moved a few steps toward the light, outlined clearly now, and he was looking up at my window. . . .

Falling back against the wall, I stared ahead blankly. I could hear my heart beating, feel it thumping against my chest.

Would he break in? Knock? Climb up to my bedroom and come through the window?

That's stupid, he didn't see you, it's too dark. He doesn't know where you are. He would have to look in every room.

By then I could get away

Or go with him

But I pushed that thought aside.

I should warn them.

Instead I stayed where I was, resting my head on

my knees, covering my ears so I would not hear Ray as he made his way inside.

He would have to look in every room.

That meant Charlie's room. Ray would leave her alone, probably. But he would look in Brian's room too.

I sat up. Ray wouldn't. Brian was too young—I calculated desperately. He was only eleven: no way. But even as I told myself that, I was grabbing my rain-soaked clothes off the floor.

I dressed quickly, then opened the door to my room. Stepping outside, I caught a glimpse of someone moving toward me down the hallway. Trembling, oddly accepting, I closed my eyes, waiting for him to arrive.

"Jeff!" Dad said. "What is it?"

I opened my eyes slowly. Dad was standing in front of me.

"I thought someone was in the house," I said after a moment.

"Who?" Dad said urgently. "You mean . . . whoever brought you here?"

"Yeah. I . . . I saw someone outside. By the porch." My voice shook.

"By the porch? Just now?" I nodded. Dad let out his breath in a long sigh. "That was me."

I stared at him.

"I just walked the perimeter of our house and every corner of the yard. There's no one out there. You don't need to feel scared."

I nodded again, not trusting my voice.

"Jeff, who brought you here?"

I shook my head. "Can I go back to my room now?"

"This man, this . . . person, is he the same one who kidnapped you?"

If I wasn't so tired, if I'd had more time to think, I might have come up with a believable story that would calm Dad and earn me a few days of peace. I briefly considered telling him I had hitchhiked to Wayne. But that would bring with it its own round of questions.

"Yes," I said. "He's the same guy."

"Who is he?" I didn't answer. "Are you scared of him?"

"No," I said, looking down. "No, not at all."

"Then why are you shaking?" Dad asked. "Why are you so pale? Why . . . "

I closed my eyes. "Please leave me alone," I whispered.

"Tell me this, just this, I need to know. . . . " I waited, knowing what he was going to ask. "Did he hurt you? Did this man hurt you?"

"No." I shook my head, attempting a smile. "No way. He just wanted a kid to stay with him, I guess. To be like his son or something . . . " Dad stared at me. "Or more like a friend, maybe. A traveling companion. He never did anything to hurt me."

"Jeff." Dad hesitated. "If he did . . . hurt you, it's all right, you know. It's not your fault. We would all know that."

Bullshit.

"Nothing happened," I said, meeting his eyes for an instant, then looking away.

"Sure," Dad said quickly. "Listen, why don't you come downstairs with me and have a snack? We can talk. . . . "

"Sorry," I said. "I really am tired."

Dad nodded. "All right. Indulge me for a second though."

I looked up at him slowly. "What?"

"I want to hug you again. I guess I can't quite believe you're really here." I didn't tell him no, and Dad came forward, enfolding me into his arms. This time I could not stop myself from shuddering.

"Are you cold?" he said, stepping back from me.

"Yeah, a little, I guess." I knew my face was red.

"I don't usually turn the heat on upstairs," Dad said, trying to sound casual. "You remember that. I'll turn it on tonight, for you."

"No, it's okay. I'm used to the cold. Can I go back to my room now?"

"Sure," he said. "But one more favor." I tensed. "Leave your door open. I want to be able to look in on you occasionally."

Squirming, I said, "I don't have any other clothes. And these"—I gestured to myself—"are wet, so . . . "

"I'll bring some things of mine for you to wear. My clothes should just about fit you now." He watched me for a moment, looking as if he wanted to say more. "Get some sleep, all right?"

I waited until he had gone into his own room to

retreat into mine. I pulled my clothes off quickly and jumped back under the covers. The bedroom door was wide open, and I did feel safer. But I knew that feeling was illusory.

Dad could talk a good game, about whether Ray "hurt" me or not, and that it was "okay" if he had. "Hurt"! He couldn't even say the words, though we both knew damn well what he meant. Nothing was "okay," or ever would be again.

THE ROOM WAS LIGHT WHEN I WOKE, AND THE nightstand clock read four o'clock. For one frightening moment I had no idea where I was. Then I remembered everything. I glanced outside the open door to my room, seeing nothing but the wall opposite, and sat up, rubbing my neck, which ached fiercely. One eye on the hallway, I leaned over the bed to grab my clothes. Feeling nothing but a damp spot on the floor, I looked over and saw that the clothes were gone. At some point, while I slept, Dad must have come in and taken them. The thought made me cringe.

Remembering what he had said about lending me some clothes, I looked around the room. A sweatshirt and a pair of jeans were draped over my desk chair, and he had left a pile of underwear and T-shirts on top of the dresser.

As Dad had said, my room was just the way I left it. Taking in the details I had been too tired to notice the night before, I saw my schoolbooks from eighth grade still on the desk, homework papers in progress tucked inside them. My knickknack shelf held the same collection of paperback books, model cars, quartz rocks, and shells. Fliers from San Francisco area sports teams festooned the walls, along with a poster that embarrassed me now, of a blond supermodel in a bikini. That particular poster was thumbtacked on the ceiling over my bed, and I wondered how anyone could have let me get away with that.

Looking away from the poster, I caught a flash of bright color through the half-open closet door. I got out of bed, pulling the sheet with me, and tapped the door lightly with my bare foot, just enough to push it open another inch or two.

My old clothes still hung neatly inside. But my shoes had been pushed to one side to make way for piles of brightly wrapped packages, some obviously from Christmases past, others from prior birthdays. Open-mouthed, I stared at the presents, feeling sick.

"Oh, Jeff, I'm sorry." It was Dad. I whirled around to face him, clutching the sheet tight around my shoulders. "Did you see the clothes I left for you?"

"Yeah," I said, giving him a tight smile. "Thanks. I'll get dressed now, okay?"

"Sure," he said, but didn't leave the room.

"Could you close the door? While I get dressed, I mean? Please."

"Sure," Dad said after a pause. "I'll be right outside." He pulled the door shut, but I didn't hear him move away from it.

I grabbed the sweatshirt off the desk chair, tugging it frantically over my head, then pulled on the jeans.

"Okay?" he asked from just outside the door.

"Yeah," I said breathlessly. He opened the door and came back into the room, smiling uncertainly, looking as embarrassed as I felt.

"My clothes almost fit you. I can't believe how you've grown. I don't know what I expected." Dad laughed awkwardly. "Connie was always after me to throw your old clothes out." I tried to smile. "I bet you're hungry."

"Kind of, yeah. I'd like to take a shower, too, if that's okay."

"You're so thin," Dad said, coming closer to me. "Why are you so thin?"

There was no safe answer. "Is it okay if I take a shower?"

"Of course. This is your house too, I told you that."

I nodded, looking away from him.

"Jeff, are you all right?" Dad said suddenly. "I know what you told me last night, and I accept that, but . . . just to be safe, maybe you should see a doctor. Just . . . just in case."

Just in case of what?

"No," I said, more forcefully than I had intended. He frowned, and I tried to paste on a reassuring smile. "I don't need to see a doctor. I'm fine. Really. Can I take my shower now?"

"Yeah," he said abruptly. "But one more thing." I

could not prevent the sigh that escaped my lips. "Take that thing off, will you?"

I looked at him, confused.

"The earring. Take it off. I'll dispose of it."

My stomach turned over and I felt the hot rush of blood to my face.

This whole time he's been looking at me and getting sick.

I reached up to my left ear and detached Ray's gift with more force than necessary. I popped the pin back in place and handed him the earring.

Don't say anything else, Dad. Just don't.

He took it in obvious distaste, leaving me alone to take my shower.

I turned the water up as hot and hard as I could stand it, letting the hard jets pound away at my shame. Then, remembering, I stepped out of the shower and locked the bathroom door. The realization that I had privacy, that Ray was not in this house and could not impose himself wherever I was, hit me with an almost physical shock.

I stayed in the shower as long as I dared. But I knew at some point I would have to face them. As a point of pride, I decided to go downstairs on my own rather than have Dad come looking for me.

Charlotte and Brian met me at the foot of the stairs. Two strangers. Brian really hadn't changed much. He was small for eleven, slim and compact. Charlotte was the real surprise. At fourteen, she looked like a shorter, curvier version of our mother, Melia. She looked so much like Melia, whom I had last seen when I was five, I couldn't help but stare. Charlotte blushed, but she did not look away from me.

"Um, Jeff," she said, trying to signal me with her eyes that something was up in the living room. I shrugged, not bothering to guess at her meaning.

"Jeff, is that you?" Connie called. "Come in here for a moment."

I stood in the archway, taking in the room at a glance. Connie was perched on the edge of the loveseat, while Dad stood next to her, a hand on her shoulder. I looked past them to the big man with the chestnut pompadour who sat on the couch across from Connie. He acknowledged my presence with a nod, watching me keenly.

"Jeff," Connie said, "this is Chief Roysten. He's with the Wayne Police Department."

"How are you, Jeff?" Roysten said.

I glanced at Dad. "I'm pretty hungry. Can this wait?"

"Yes, he needs to eat," Dad said.

"Just a few questions, then," the chief said.

Connie stood. "I'm taking Charlie and Brian out to get something for dinner. Chinese okay with everyone?"

In the general agreement that followed I entered the room, taking the seat Connie had left.

"All right," Roysten said, leaning forward, staring at me. "How did you get here?"

I looked to Dad again, but his expression was unreadable. "How did I get to Wayne, you mean?"

"Yep." Roysten nodded. "How'd you get to Wayne?"

"Um . . . the guy I was with, he just . . . he decided to bring me home, I guess."

Roysten said nothing, watching me for an uncomfortably long time.

"I don't know where he is now," I added.

"How long were you with him?"

"I don't know. However long I was gone, I guess."

"Were you boyfriends with him, Jeff?" the chief asked earnestly. I could hear the smile behind his words and I sat very still.

"What kind of a question is that to ask him?" Dad raged, walking over to Roysten, who stood to meet him.

"Hey," Roysten said. "I know it's tough, but let's get the cards on the table here."

Dad paced a little, then sat down abruptly on the easy chair between the two couches. He rubbed his thumb back and forth against his mouth in a gesture of anger that I remembered.

The chief sat down again, then leaned over the arm of the couch. He pulled a green lawn bag off the floor, setting it down with a thud on the table between us.

"What is that?" I asked tensely.

"Well, it's a lawn bag," Roysten said. "I was hoping you could tell me if this bag means anything to you."

"No," I said quickly, looking at Dad. I was telling the truth—I didn't know what Roysten was talking about. All I knew was that looking at the bag made me feel ashamed.

"You don't know what's in here?" Roysten asked. I shook my head.

Taking his time, he shook the bag open, reaching deep inside. His eyes on me, Roysten pulled out a sleeveless San Francisco 49'ers jersey, tossing it onto the coffee table. He reached in again and pulled out a battered running shoe with a sock stuffed inside it.

I had thought there was nothing Ray could do to shock me anymore. I was wrong.

"Okay," I said. "I get it, you don't have to . . . "

Roysten turned the bag upside down, shaking it out. Another shoe, a loose sock, and a pair of cutoff denim shorts spilled out onto the coffee table.

"All right," Dad said. "Jesus Christ, you don't have to turn this into a show. Jeff, these are the clothes you were wearing the day you disappeared. Aren't they?"

"Yes," I said, amazed at how calm I sounded.

"Someone set that bag against the front door last night. Connie found it this morning when she went out to get the paper."

"He came back," I said quietly.

"*He* did . . . or was it you who put the clothes out there?" Roysten asked.

"Me?" I looked at Roysten, then Dad. "No. I haven't seen those clothes since . . . "

My face flamed.

Since Ray took them off me.

Dad stood up. Without looking at me, he touched my hair briefly. I ducked my head, staring at the floor.

"Roysten, that's enough," Dad said. "We'll take it from here."

"Hey," Roysten said, "we're just getting started."

"No," Dad said. "Your part in this is finished, at least as far as Jeff is concerned." He paused. "I've got someone coming up from the FBI. You can talk to him later if you're still interested."

Roysten stood. "You still want those patrols, don't you?"

Dad nodded, standing right in front of Roysten, forcing the man either to move back or physically confront him. Roysten moved.

"Yeah. I still want the patrols."

"I'll keep sending 'em then," the chief said as Dad ushered him out.

As their voices faded, Roysten's cajoling, Dad's cool and grim, I wondered why neither of them had mentioned the smell of the things piled on the table. It was not possible they hadn't noticed it. I swallowed hard, tasting bile in the back of my throat.

Gagging, I picked the bag up off the floor. Holding it open against the coffee table, I shoved the stuff back inside, feeling contaminated with every new item I touched.

I held the bag out from my body, no idea what to do next. Then I remembered the laundry room. When I lived here before, we had shared the chores around the house, and once in a while I had done the laundry.

I hurried to the small room off the kitchen. A wet load of laundry was still in the washer, and I dumped my things inside with it, then the bag too. I tossed in a measuring cup of Tide, shut the lid, turned the timing dial to Heavy Soil and pushed the button to start the cycle. As water began to fill the tub, I leaned heavily against the machine, trying to catch my breath.

"What are you doing?" Dad said. I stood up, turning to face him, my heart racing. My hands tingled, filthy. I held them out far from my sides, knowing I had to wash them before I touched anything else.

"Jeff?" He sounded bewildered.

"I'm washing the clothes."

"You're . . . washing the clothes," he repeated, running a hand through his hair. "You mean the clothes from the bag?"

"Yes," I said impatiently. "They were dirty. I had to wash them."

"Jeff . . . " Dad hesitated. "The police, not Roysten, the FBI, they might need those things. As evidence."

"I had to wash them."

"Why?" Dad asked, looking at me as though I was crazy.

I stared back at him. "Because they were dirty."

"Jeff, someone is coming up to talk with you this evening," Dad announced as Connie dished the Chinese food into bowls along the table. "An FBI agent out of San Francisco. His name is Dave Stephens. He's been on your case almost since the day you disappeared."

"I don't want to talk to anyone," I said, ignoring the food. "I'm here, isn't that enough?" My stomach growled so loudly Brian laughed, then looked around as though he'd be punished for it.

"No," Dad said. "For everyone's safety, you have to talk. You'll like Dave. He's very gentle."

The word was an insult. "*Gentle*? Shit." I pushed my chair back.

"Jeff." Dad motioned me back to the table. "Relax. I'm trying to say that Dave is nothing like Roysten. He's a good man." I watched him. "Eat your food. Go on."

"I'm not talking," I warned him.

He nodded toward the food. "Eat."

I hesitated, but I was too hungry to argue with him.

Charlie and Brian had already served themselves, so I did the same, ladling a portion of beef with broccoli onto my plate. Self-consciously, I took a bite. It was delicious, the best food I ever remembered tasting, and I dove in, eating ravenously, not looking up again until my plate was clean. I looked at Connie, not sure how to ask for more.

"Try some cashew chicken next," she urged me, smiling, "or just help yourself, hon. You're the guest of honor."

"Go ahead," Dad said, too heartily. I scooped a good-sized portion onto my plate from each of the steaming bowls in the center of the table, then topped that off with a huge dollop of rice.

"I'm sorry, I haven't eaten in a while," I said after I finished, sitting back, feeling a little sick. I wiped my mouth with the back of my sleeve, then reached, too late, for a napkin. Dad caught my arm.

"Hey, you're with your family. This is your food too." He paused, then cleared his throat. "When did you eat last?"

My arm tingled where Dad held it. I looked away, and he released me.

"Sometime yesterday."

"Where?"

"You said we could wait 'til that guy got here."

"Jeff, just tell us if we have anything to fear," Connie said. "He came to our house. Twice, at least." She shivered, rubbing her arms.

"He's not coming back," I said flatly. "He dropped

me off, he dropped the clothes off. There's no reason for him to come back now."

"But do you know that for sure?" Connie asked. I just stared at her. "I mean . . . who is he? What—"

"Connie," Dad murmured. She shut her mouth abruptly, looking down.

"I'm done eating," I said. "Thanks." I looked past Connie to Dad. "Can I go to my room now?"

"But we have ice cream," Brian said, smiling shyly at me. "I asked Mom if we could get some, after we got the Chinese. I remembered you used to like chocolate chip. You still do, don't you?"

"Come on, Jeff, help me get it," Charlotte said, tugging lightly at my shoulder. I followed her to the kitchen.

She nodded me toward the fridge and began to get the bowls out of the cabinet. Charlie's sleek black cat, Jack, crouched near the door leading out to the backyard. He looked up at me sideways, suspicious.

I knelt a few feet from him, holding out a cupped hand. "Hi, boy. Remember me?" Jack made a small noise, somewhere between a meow and a purr, and came to me. I rubbed the side of his face, grinning.

"I missed this guy," I said, almost to myself. I picked up the cat and rubbed my chin against his soft head. He leaned against me and began purring loudly. "He remembers me!" I looked up at Charlie, unguarded for the first time. She was leaning against the counter, hands over her face, crying soundlessly.

I stood up, uncomfortable, setting the cat down.

Charlie lowered her arms and gulped once, swallowing a sob.

"I want to hug you," she said. "Can I? If it wouldn't make you feel weird."

Trapped, I submitted with a shrug.

She released me quickly, reaching for a paper towel to mop her face. I busied myself scooping the ice cream into dishes.

"Hey, what are you kids doing?" Dad called from the dining room. "We're starving out here!"

"We're coming," Charlie called back, smiling at me.

She carried out two bowls of ice cream and I took the other three. Brian passed us, heading into the kitchen with the empty food cartons, Connie behind him with a pile of dirty dishes.

Once we'd all sat down again, there was a knock at the door.

"I'll get it!" Brian yelled, and sprang up.

"No, you won't," Dad said, jumping up to follow him. I let my spoon clink down in the bowl.

"I'm sure that's Dave," Connie said. But she watched after Dad, cocking her head to listen as he opened the door. A man's voice rang out in greeting and she nodded. "It's him."

Brian ran back in and sat down. Dad and a rumpled-looking man somewhere in his forties followed him.

The man from the FBI was huge. Dad was six feet tall, but this man dwarfed him. He outweighed Dad too, by a good eighty pounds, his potbelly straining against the white button-down shirt he wore under a wrinkled suit jacket. His full face was framed by a head of bushy brown hair. He noticed me staring at him and looked back at me, his deep-set brown eyes peering into mine. I looked down quickly.

Dad's here, they're all here, there's no reason to be scared.

But I was.

"Dave, you know Connie," Dad said, gesturing toward her. Connie stood to shake Stephens's hand.

"It's been too long," she said, smiling, a slight edge to her voice.

"Always a pleasure, Connie," he said, clasping her hand briefly.

"Brian . . . " Dad nodded in his direction.

"Sure, Brian and I are old friends," Stephens said.

"Hi," Charlie said shyly, when Dad didn't introduce her.

"Is this Charlotte? I haven't seen you for a while. What a pretty girl! Ken, you've got a good-looking family here."

What was this guy's act?

I glanced at Dad, who stood slightly behind Stephens. His face was red and it looked as though he was holding back tears. Panicked, I looked for an escape route.

Stephens stuck his big hand in my face. "You must be Jeff," he said. I looked at his hand and then down at my plate.

"I'd love some of that . . . what is it, chocolate

chip?" Stephens said, pulling his hand back smoothly. "If you've got any to spare."

"Of course," Connie said. "I'll get some for you." She stopped by Dad on her way into the kitchen, squeezing his shoulder and whispering something in his ear. He nodded.

"I'll get you a chair, Dave," Dad said, his voice choked. He left the room quickly.

Stephens stood over the three of us, his eyes still on me. The room was silent until Brian piped up, "We just had Chinese food. It was good. Jeff ate most of it, though. He said he hasn't eaten since yesterday."

"Shut up," I snapped. "Shut the fuck up." Brian turned his shocked face my way, eyes wide. Charlie could have been his twin.

"Everything all right in here?" Dad asked as he walked back into the room, carrying the extra dining room chair.

"Sure, we're fine," Stephens said. "Ah, great," he sighed as he sank into the plush chair. Nothing but the best for the Hart family.

Connie returned with a heaping dish of ice cream and placed it before Stephens. "Dave, how about a real meal? We have a casserole left over from last night, or I could make you a sandwich."

"No, thanks, the ice cream's plenty," he said. "I grabbed a burger in some little town on the way up. Oak something."

"Oakdale? Main street, not much else?" Dad said.

"Yeah, that's the place. Kind of a nice change after the Bay Area, but I don't think I'd want to live there."

Stephens ate his ice cream as if that was the reason he was here. He and Dad spoke to each other with an easiness that made them sound like colleagues. I sat across from them sullenly, watching my ice cream melt, my stomach protesting its unaccustomed load of Chinese food.

"Well," Stephens said finally, smiling, turning to me. "Let's get started. Jeff . . . " He stopped at the look on my face. "Ken, is there a room we can use?"

"Of course," Dad said. "There's my office, or you could go upstairs—"

I broke in. "Look, I'm sorry he wasted his time coming here, but I have nothing to say."

Stephens smiled, leaning back in his chair. "A bowl of chocolate chip ice cream is never wasted, Jeff."

"Oh, that's funny," I said. "I'm sixteen, not six!" Then I stared down at the table, afraid of the anger I had shown.

"Look," Stephens said quietly. "You've just come home. You're disoriented, you want to sleep, you want everyone to quit looking at you. Right?" Reluctantly, I nodded. "All that is going to happen. Things are going to calm down. You're going to live a regular life again. But, Jeff . . . "

Something in his voice compelled me to look at him.

"Before that can happen, you have work to do. Now,

I don't need extensive testimony tonight, but we do need to establish a few basic facts."

I moved my chair back a little and sighed.

"It was a man who kidnapped you, yes?" I nodded. "Was he the one who brought you home last night?"

"Yeah."

Stephens took out a small notepad and pen. "Describe his vehicle: make, model and license number."

"I don't know. It was new. He just showed up with it. I don't know the plate number."

"Car? Truck? Van?" Stephens held the pen, ready to write.

"He's driving a car," I said. "Dark-colored. Maybe black."

"Yeah?" Stephens squinted at me. "And?"

"It's just a car, nothing special about it. I don't know, all right?" I threw my napkin down on the table and stood up.

Dad stood with me. "Sit down, Jeff," he ordered.

I hesitated, then sat.

"Let's start over," Stephens said. "When you said he 'showed up' with the car, 'showed up' where? Were you staying at a house, or—"

"No, it was a street corner. Some city around L.A. I don't know where exactly. He drove me there in the van, told me to wait and came back with this car. Maybe he stole it or something. I couldn't ask him, you know."

"Wait a minute," Dad said, his voice slow, considering. "You were alone on a street corner somewhere? I don't understand. Why didn't you run away? Get help?"

I shrugged uncomfortably, realizing I had caught myself in a lie that sounded more suspicious than the truth.

"Jeff." Stephens's voice was intense. "What van?"

I looked up at him, suddenly alert. "Van? There was no van."

"You said he drove you to this street corner in 'the van'."

I stared at him, speechless, then tried to recover. "I made the whole thing up, okay? No street corner, no van."

He stared back at me for so long I began to squirm. "What?" I asked finally.

"What are you trying to pull here?" Stephens's voice was quiet.

"Nothing! God, why don't you just . . . " I paused, trying to control my voice. "I'm here, okay?" I looked around the table at all of them. "I'm here. So why do we have to get into a whole big thing about—"

"Who is this guy?" Stephens said, unmoved. "Who are we talking about?"

"I don't know his name," I said, glaring at him. Stephens cocked an eyebrow. "I don't! He went by different names." Brian was staring at me open-mouthed, as if I was the best detective show he'd ever seen.

"Yeah? What name did he go by most often?"

"Harold," I lied. "John. Al. There were others."

"What does he look like? How old is he?"

"I don't know. He's just average. Just an average, middle-aged guy."

"Uh-huh. And where's he heading?"

"I'm not sure. He said he wanted to travel. He mentioned Nevada once."

Stephens threw his pen onto the table between us. The notebook followed. "So we're looking for a middle-aged male answering to Harold, John, or Al, in an unknown car heading for parts unknown. Maybe Nevada. If you're going to lie, you can do better than that."

I just shook my head, looking down at the table.

"Jeff," Dad pleaded, "come on now. Talk to Dave."

"I tried talking to him," I flared, looking sideways at Dad. "He doesn't want to listen."

"You're not telling the truth," Stephens said. He sounded disgusted. "You're protecting this guy."

"I'm not protecting *anyone*," I said, dangerously close to tears. I stood, the need fierce to get away from him, from all of them.

Dad reached out for me. I backstepped away, stumbling, banging my hip against the table.

"All right. All right," he said, to me or Stephens I didn't know. "That's enough for now."

Upstairs, I stared at myself in the mirror, despising the large green eyes, the high cheekbones, the full mouth, the features that had marked me "beautiful" in Ray's eyes. I flipped my hair out of my eyes, the thick, silky dark blond hair he loved to touch. I hated it. I hated myself.

Dᴀᴅ ᴡᴏᴋᴇ ᴍᴇ ᴀᴛ ᴛᴇɴ ᴛʜᴇ ɴᴇxᴛ ᴍᴏʀɴɪɴɢ, shaking my shoulder gently. I looked up at him bleary-eyed. I had sat up most of the night, allowing myself to fall into sleep only as dawn approached.

"Time to get up, Jeff," he said, smiling. "Come downstairs and have some breakfast."

"Good morning, honey," Connie greeted me as I walked into the kitchen. I noticed the fine lines under her eyes, more than I remembered from before.

"Morning, Connie. You look tired," I said, then blushed. "I'm sorry, I mean, you look good, just tired." I stood awkwardly against the counter, suddenly shy with her.

Connie smiled. "Actually, this morning I'm not. Usually on Saturdays I have to get up at five-thirty to take Charlie to her job at the stables. But Dave drove her today, and I slept in 'til eight. Can I get you something?"

"You don't have to. I don't know. Cereal's okay." She nodded and brought down a box of Rice Chex from one of the cabinets. "Charlie has a job?"

"Yes, she works at the fairgrounds weekend mornings grooming and exercising the horses. Charlie went out and got the job on her own. We were shocked. She's usually so quiet and . . . moody. The job has been wonderful for her, though."

"How long has she worked there?" I asked, taking the bowl of cereal from Connie.

"About three months, I guess. Since the end of summer. Vin Perini works there too, weekday mornings mostly, but sometimes on weekends with Charlie. She's so shy when she sees him. It's cute." Connie laughed. "Oh, she'd kill me if she heard me say that. Jeff, aren't you hungry?"

I had set the bowl on the counter without taking a bite. I could not remember the last time I had thought of Vinny. Getting used to my family again was one thing. But thinking of Vinny, of the complications of getting to know him again, of the process of reacquainting myself with kids my own age, school . . . the thought of the weeks and months to come overwhelmed me.

"Are you okay?" I realized Connie had spoken twice to me without my answering. She touched my arm.

"Yeah. I guess I'm still tired."

"Have you eaten yet?" Dad strode into the room. "No? Bring your bowl into the office. Dave wants to talk to you." I didn't move. "Come on, there's no better time. Charlie's out, Connie's taking Brian shopping with her. Let's get this over with."

Wordlessly I followed him to his office. The room looked the same as I remembered it, with the addition of some embarrassingly large photos of me. I lingered in front of one. It was me right after pitching a no-hitter in a Little League championship game. Vinny was in the foreground among my teammates congratulating me.

Dad laughed awkwardly. "Nice, huh? I bought a copy from the *Telegraph* and had it enlarged. That was some day, remember?"

"Yeah . . . " I said, trailing off, disturbed by the picture. Stephens walked into the room.

"We'll have to get some new pictures of you," Dad said. "You . . . you've grown up since then."

Stephens cleared his throat. "Ken, you mind getting me some coffee?"

"Coffee?" Dad hesitated a moment, watching me. "Sure."

I watched him go, not sure whether I was relieved or scared to be free of him.

"Would it be easier on you if your dad wasn't here for this?" Stephens's voice was quiet.

I put the cereal bowl on an end table and sat down, avoiding his eyes. "I'm not going to say anything, so it doesn't matter."

"But if you do say something," Stephens said patiently, "would you prefer he not be here?"

I shrugged, trying to hide my panic. Stephens left the room. I covered my ears, not wanting to hear the explanation he would give to Dad.

I lowered my hands quickly as Stephens lumbered back into the room. He pulled Dad's office chair over to the couch where I sat and perched on it, towering over me.

"First, please call me Dave. Everyone does."

I glanced up at him. The man looked like a movie version of a bodyguard—the big, dumb guy who backs up the slick villain. I held on to that image to keep my fear at bay.

"You're from the FBI?"

"That's right."

"And you let everyone call you Dave? Or is it just crime victims?"

He smiled wearily at me. "Okay. Forget the pleasantries. Was any of that story true last night?"

"Yes," I admitted. "But . . . " I looked away, laughing a little. "The thing is, I'm not going to talk. The guy's not coming back, okay? He left me off, I'm here, end of story."

"Uh-uh," Stephens said, still smiling. "An awful lot of people expended a lot of time and energy on you over the past few years. They want some return on their investment. So do I."

I looked at him as if he was insane. "What are you talking about? You mean people tried to find me and all that?"

"Yep. All that. Ask your dad sometime."

"Yeah, well, I never saw any of it," I told him hotly, then looked away, frowning.

"Why not? He keep you confined, or what?"

I looked back at the man. "Hey, I'm not stupid. You're not going to trip me up that way. I'm not talking, so you can just go back—"

"I know you're not stupid. In fact, I understand you used to be the perfect kid. Polite, respectful, good student, star athlete . . . " He ticked the qualities off one by one on his fingers.

I squirmed. "Is there something wrong with that?"

He smiled a little. "The perfect kid with the perfect life. That's what your dad kept insisting. No problems at school, none at home, no reason to run."

"You thought I ran away?"

"I came onto your case the third day," Stephens said. "And only because Ken made such a stink. There's a knee-jerk response in law enforcement that kids over ten who go missing are probably runaways. Here you were, almost fourteen, so . . . "

I felt sick. Here was my fear made flesh. "Is that what you thought?"

"I'm not big into knee-jerk responses." Stephens gave me a quick smile. "But if you didn't run, what happened to you? You were just *gone*. One of the most frustrating cases I ever worked."

I watched him, not sure where he was going with this.

"So . . . where were you?"

I shrugged, my stomach churning.

"Aside from everything else, I'm curious as hell.

You know we never came up with one solid lead about you? I finally figured you were so far underground that unless someone confessed, we were never going to find you."

"What do you mean, 'underground'?" I asked. "Dead?"

He nodded. "Dead—or dead to the world, anyway. Was I right?"

"I don't know what you want me to say."

"Simple. Where have you been for the last two and a half years?" I was silent. "Try this then: who kidnapped you?"

I looked down, shaking my head.

"What if he comes back again?"

"He won't."

"You sure? He came back once already to drop off your clothes."

"He's done. He won't come back."

"You know something, you're right," Stephens said slowly. "He probably won't come back for you. Brian, though, he's what, eleven?"

"Don't," I said, knowing what he was doing, reacting anyway.

"Face it, Jeff. If it's not Brian, it'll be some other kid. You want to be responsible for that?"

I stared at him, furious. "It's not my job to catch him, it's yours. I'm not responsible for what he does."

"You're the last known contact with this man. I'm not leaving until you tell me how to find him."

"I don't know how to find him. I can't help you." I looked down, miserable, my arms folded across my chest, one foot tapping nervously.

The silence went on so long I had to look up. Stephens was staring at me, looking disgusted, and angry too.

"I'm sorry," I said, shuddering involuntarily. I moved to get up, to leave him. Stephens reacted immediately, pushing his chair forward, knocking my legs apart with his own, clamping his hands on my thighs and leaning into me.

"You're not getting out of it this easy," he hissed, inches from my face. "Now come on. What's the man's name?"

Frozen, I could only blink at him. Just as I saw his face soften into a kind of regret, I was able to let out a strangled cry. Stephens pulled back immediately and stood up, cursing.

Dad ran into the room so fast I knew he must have been just outside, listening. He came swiftly to my side.

"What the hell is wrong with you?" he yelled, and I shivered before I realized he was talking to Stephens. "If you treat him that way again," Dad continued, his voice quiet now, "I'll take the kid and disappear and your case can go to hell."

"Look, I'm sorry," Stephens said. "If we had the time, he could work this through at his own pace. But we don't. Jeff, the guy dropped you off Thursday night.

It's Saturday morning now. Your kidnapper has had a full day, and part of another, to start this whole process again. Take some other kid, ruin his life, ruin his family's life, maybe kill him this time. We've got to stop him. You know that."

I swallowed hard. "I can't talk about him."

"You're embarrassed about the sex. I understand that." Stephens's tone was gentle now.

I hid my face from him, from both of them. "There was no sex," I mumbled.

"Well, I don't believe you. But let's set that aside for now. I need to know who kidnapped you. The best description you can give me. I don't need to know anything more now than who he is and how to find him."

Dad squeezed my shoulder. Breathing deeply, I raised my head to look at Stephens. "He goes by 'Ray.' None of those other names I told you were true."

"Okay," Stephens said, sitting down again, a good distance from me this time. "Is Ray his first or last name?"

"I don't know. That's what he told me to call him, so . . . "

Stephens nodded. "Do you know where he's heading?"

"No. He did mention Nevada once, Las Vegas, but . . . I don't know."

"Where did he keep you?" I shook my head. Stephens watched me calmly, notepad out, poised to write.

"No. I can't say that." I kept my head down, but I

was serious, no matter what they did to me. "I can't . . . " I dared to look up at Stephens. "I won't."

He sighed, thought about it for a moment, then nodded. "What does Ray look like? How old is he?"

"I don't know how old he is," I said, irritated, trapped. "Maybe forty."

"What does he look like?"

"He has long black hair. Past his collar. Brown eyes. He's tall, about six feet."

"Body type?"

"Ray's thin, but he has muscles. He lifts weights." I flushed at that bit of information, cursing myself for giving Stephens more than he'd asked for. He remained expressionless, taking notes as I spoke.

"Does Ray have any scars? Any identifying marks?"

"He has a little scar above his left eyebrow. When he gets mad, it stands out white against his skin." I saw that my hands were shaking and clasped them together in my lap.

"How did he bring you here? Car, van, what?"

"He has a Lexus. It's black. I don't know the license number." Stephens looked at me. "I don't!"

"Did he tell you anything about himself? His family, where he grew up, any personal details?"

"He said he used to be a lawyer. He'd laugh about it." Dad released my shoulder, staring down at me. "He talked about his ex-wife a few times. Not her name. Just . . . just that he'd been married once."

Stephens nodded. "Fine. That'll do for a start. Anything else, Jeff?"

"Yeah." I looked at him but the message was for Dad. "I know what you think about Ray, and you're wrong. He never touched me."

Stephens nodded, turning to Dad. "I want Jeff to come down to the city to look at mugshots. Why don't you bring the whole family and we'll put you up at a nice hotel? This situation will be easier to control if you're out of town, isolated together in a safe place."

"I can protect my family," Dad burst out, so suddenly I flinched.

"I know you can," Stephens said quietly. "I'm not just talking about Ray here. The press will be around soon enough, and all the relatives and anyone else who ever knew Jeff will be wanting to see him. He's not ready for that yet."

I ducked my head, embarrassed, hiding my face from both of them.

"All right," Dad said angrily. "We'll go to the Bay Area then."

Stephens made the arrangements by phone for us to stay in a suite at the San Francisco Hilton. We formed a two car tandem for the three hour commute to the city, Stephens leading the way. I was silent the entire time, sunk in disbelief that I had broken so easily to his questioning.

As soon as we hit town, Stephens insisted I go to the FBI building with him. He directed Dad to stay at the Hilton to "get the family settled" which I figured was a ploy to get me alone again.

"The FBI offices are over there," Stephens said, maneuvering his way through the late afternoon weekend traffic. "See? That skyscraper that looks like black steel. There should be a few people working today, but it won't be crowded."

"I don't care," I said tightly.

Stephens pulled into the underground parking garage connected to the FBI building and motored into a space marked with his name.

"I know I pushed you hard back at the house," he

said as we got out of the car. "I hope you understand why I did it."

"Sure. You wanted to teach me a lesson or some other shit like that."

"No," he said, staring at me over the top of the car. "No, Jeff, I didn't want to teach you a lesson, in particular."

"You wanted to scare me then."

Stephens nodded, a touch reluctantly. "I wanted to shock you into telling the truth. I'm sorry I had to do it that way."

"You liked doing it, I could tell," I shot back at him. "You had your hands all over me." He watched me for a moment, expressionless, then took off walking through the lot. After a moment, I followed him.

Stephens's office was cluttered but organized. His desk was stacked high with folders divided into neat piles, and metal filing cabinets as tall as I was lined one wall. The wall opposite held posters of missing children, tacked up and spaced so neatly they resembled a mural. I approached the wall with a sick fascination, stopping when I saw myself there, the same poster I had seen on the convenience store window.

I stared at the poster, absorbing the details I could not before. The boy in the poster was blond, clean-cut, grinning widely and wearing a blue polo shirt that I suddenly remembered as my favorite from that year. He weighed 120 pounds, stood 5´6˝ and had a small scar on his right hand. I fingered that scar absently—Charlie had accidentally slammed a car door on my hand once—until I sensed Stephens's presence behind me.

"We're going to have to list you as 'found' now," he said, sounding happy.

I stepped around him carefully, heading for a battered green couch by the door. At the last moment, I realized I did not want Stephens towering over me again, so I perched on the arm of the couch.

"Did you know Ray was bringing you back?" Stephens asked, leaning against his desk now, all business.

I shook my head. "He didn't tell me where we were going, or why."

"Did he drop you off right away or did he hang around for a while?"

I stiffened. "What do you mean 'hang around'?"

"Why does that upset you, Jeff?" Stephens opened his eyes wide.

"It doesn't!" I flared. "Just . . . he left me in Wayne, okay? That's all."

Stephens pointed at me. "Ray didn't just leave you and drive off. He stayed around long enough to drop off your clothes. The same clothes you were wearing when you disappeared."

I almost laughed. "Yeah, I know."

"Did you know he was going to do that?"

"No." I shifted, feeling prickles of heat up and down my arms. "I came here to look through photos for you. Don't ask me anything else."

"Eventually you'll have to say what happened between you and Ray. You might as well start now."

"Nothing happened. He kidnapped me. That's all."

"Why did he kidnap you?" Stephens asked. "You told your dad Ray wanted a traveling companion. Is that true?"

I stared at him, betrayed. Goddamn Dad.

"Look, I understand that you're embarrassed."

"I'm not embarrassed," I said through gritted teeth. "I have no reason to be embarrassed."

Stephens nodded. "That's true. You have no reason to be embarrassed. I hope you'll understand that one day."

I looked away from him, confused.

Stephens stood, gesturing toward a stack of papers on his desk. "My assistant pulled these mugshots for us. All of the men have been arrested for kidnapping a child within the last ten years in California, and all of them roughly match your description of Ray. I want you to go through them carefully. All right?" He waited for my nod. "I'm going to go out and play with the computers for a while. Give me a yell when you're done."

Once Stephens was out of the room I hesitated, feeling a strange reluctance to delve into the pile, as though seeing all the men would make me a part of what they had done.

I looked carefully at the first dozen or so photos. But soon the staring dark eyes, black hair and blank faces began to run into one another. Only an especially bizarre-looking man or an inappropriate expression made me look twice. Halfway through, I came to a convict who'd bared his teeth for the camera in an unconvincing imitation of a grin, his eyes half-lidded and head tilted back. I flipped the photo up and read the crime sheet clipped to the back. The man had been convicted of kidnapping and raping his five-year-old nephew. I threw the picture down on Stephens's desk, sickened. I read the rap sheets of the next five men: all had served time for sexual crimes as well as kidnapping.

I stood motionless for a moment, then swept the pictures off the desk, knocking over two of Stephens's folders in the process. My fury turned to fear when I saw the mess I had created. I knelt, grabbing the papers off the floor, my heart racing as I watched for Stephens. Without looking at the stack of papers I had collected, I divided it in half, placing each section randomly inside the folders. Next I picked up the mugshots, tapped them into a neat pile, and set them back in the center of Stephens's desk.

When Stephens returned fifteen minutes later, I was sitting on the arm of the couch, just as he had left me.

"Through already?" he said after a moment.

"I didn't recognize anyone," I said flatly.

"How hard did you look?"

"Why is every man in there some kind of sick rapist pervert?" I stumbled over my words. "I told you Ray isn't like that."

"I think he is," Stephens said calmly. "The longer I'm around you, the more strongly I believe that."

I dared to look at him. "You think you know me. You're wrong."

"Actually," Stephens said, "I don't know you. But I do know guys like Ray." Our eyes held for a moment, and then I looked away.

Our suite at the Hilton was near the top floor. Connie and Dad had set up in the master bedroom, with Charlie, Brian and I ranged out in the spacious living room.

I flopped into the daybed by the window, far away from where the others would sleep. Charlie chose one of the long velvet couches and Brian settled onto the rollaway cot.

After Connie triple-locked the door, even setting a chair against it, she hugged Brian, wished Charlie good night and came over and stood by my bed. I knew she was waiting for a signal from me, but I kept my eyes closed. Finally Connie kissed me lightly on the forehead. I restrained myself from wiping it off, but I turned over and buried my head in the pillow.

Good night. Turn off the goddamn lights.

After a moment, she did, retreating to the room where Dad and Stephens were discussing my performance. I wrapped the pillow around my head so I wouldn't hear anything, blanking out Charlie's voice calling softly to me.

I DIDN'T SLEEP UNTIL I SAW THE FIRST CRACK OF sun through the hotel drapes. The next thing I knew, Dad was shaking me awake.

"We're ordering room service," he said. "What do you want for breakfast?" His light brown eyes were intense as he knelt beside me. I watched him, speechless, wondering what Stephens had said to him the night before.

Dad cleared his throat. "How about some eggs—an omelet, something to get you going? I'm taking you shopping today after breakfast."

"Can I have toast and coffee?" I wasn't hungry at all.

"Coffee?" He frowned, then shrugged. "Okay."

I was sullen in the car, waiting for him to ask me about Ray or about what had happened with Stephens. But Dad was quiet, driving fast through mostly empty streets to the downtown shopping area.

We hit The Gap just as the store was opening so there were hardly any customers. Still, the floor-to-ceiling glass walls, bright white lights and mirrors everywhere made me feel on display. I grabbed two pairs of jeans and a couple of long-sleeved T-shirts off display tables near the door.

"Is this okay, Dad?" He was watching me like a hawk. A salesclerk hovered, scoping me out with almost the same intensity.

"He'll need some sweaters," she said.

Dad frowned at her, then nodded. "Pick out a couple of sweaters, Jeff."

"Green would go good with his eyes," the girl suggested, her own blue eyes gleaming. She was somewhere in her twenties, tall with long black hair and a nametag that read Michelle. "And turquoise would bring out those flecks of blue. He has the kind of eyes that can look deep blue or deep green, depending on what he wears." Resting her weight on one leg, she looked me over head to toe. I felt my face start to burn and I looked imploringly at Dad.

"Miss, when we decide, we'll find you." His voice was cold. Once she was gone, he smiled at me. "I think you have a fan."

I felt so awkward I could barely raise my eyes. "Can we go?"

Dad hesitated. "Sure. But I want to get this done. Pick out a couple of sweaters and a jacket, try them on and we'll get out of here."

We were walking out of The Gap when I remembered. "Dad, I didn't really need a new coat. I have that leather jacket. It's really warm, and I just got it. . . . "

"You don't need any of those things now. After we get you some shoes, you're going to dump the ones you're wearing." I looked sideways at him. "I don't want anything around that reminds you of that man."

"Okay," I said softly, but my stomach lurched as I realized the impossibility of his statement.

Dad steered me into a Foot Locker and bought a brand-new version of the white Filas I had been wearing. As we left the store, he crossed over to a garbage container by the curb, slamming my old shoes into it with an intensity that made me cringe.

"What else do you need?" he asked, walking back to me with a smile. "Can you think of anything? Another pair of shoes? How about something fun—a CD player? Some in-line skates or—"

"I'm okay, really." I didn't want to go into any other store. The sun had made its way high over the tops of the tallest buildings, and I was starting to feel warm. I remembered how hot San Francisco could get in December. Holding a hand up to shield my eyes, I looked at the sky.

"Sunglasses!" Dad said. "How about a pair of sunglasses? There's a good place a few blocks over. . . . "

It was only eleven o'clock on a Sunday morning but the streets were beginning to crowd up. I walked close to Dad, our differences set aside in my need to feel safe. I flinched every time someone's eyes flicked over me, moving even closer to Dad whenever there was a possibility someone was going to bump into me on the sidewalk. Dad strolled along, glancing at me often, smiling.

"Can we stop somewhere for a minute?" I finally asked him.

Dad stopped walking, pulling me over to the recessed window of a stationery store to let people by. "Are you tired? Hungry? You hardly touched your breakfast."

I shook my head. "No, it's just . . . can we go back now?"

"Back to the hotel?" I nodded. "Why? Is something wrong?"

"I think people know who I am," I said. "They keep staring. . . . " My face burned. Dad placed his hand against my forehead. I felt too weak to deny him, laying my head against the store's glass window.

"Your skin is clammy," Dad said, frowning. "What's wrong? Do you feel sick?"

I'm scared. I don't want to be around all these people. I feel like a freak. They know about me.

"I guess I'm still tired."

Dad shook his head. "We can't give in to that. You have things you need to accomplish. You're just going to have to keep putting one foot in front of the other."

Thanks for the pep talk, Dad.

If I had the nerve, I would have sneered at him. He watched me closely for a moment, then relaxed.

"Come on. Let's get a soft drink or something."

We sat in an outdoor cafe, Dad drinking iced coffee, me on my second Pepsi. I had drained the first as soon as the waiter had set it in front of me.

"Better?" Dad asked me finally after we had sat in silence for some minutes.

I shrugged. "Yeah, I guess."

"What was making you nervous out there?"

"The crowds," I said quickly, glancing up at him.

"The crowds," he repeated. "Did this man . . . did you ever see anyone else? Did he take you out?"

I clasped my drink tightly, rubbing at the drops of moisture with my thumbs. "Please stop asking me questions like that."

"Questions like what?" he threw back at me, so fast I jumped. The waiter came over to leave our bill on the table. He was young, maybe five years older than me, short and fit, his dark hair cut close to the skull. He winked at me and I looked away quickly, hoping Dad hadn't seen.

"I don't want to talk about it," I said. "You're pushing me . . . "

Dad took a deep breath. "That's not fair. I've been very patient with you. I'm doing my best not to push." He held up a hand as I started to respond. "As long as you make the effort to catch this guy, the rest of it can wait."

"There is no 'rest of it,' " I said, not looking at him. "Can we go back to the hotel now?"

Dad waited, then shook his head. "No. Not yet."

"People keep staring at me," I said, hoping to convince him. "Maybe they've seen me on the news or something."

He shook his head. "We've done a good job of keeping the press away from you. They don't know what you look like now." Dad cleared his throat. "The thing is, your appearance is striking. Your mother—Melia—was a beautiful woman. You've always resembled her, and now with your height . . . you're a beautiful young man. That's why people are looking at you."

Red-faced, I stared down at the table.

"Hey," he said, reaching across the table to lay his hand on mine, "I'm not trying to embarrass you. The way you look is not your fault."

My fault.

"As soon as we get you a decent haircut, the effect will be less . . . " Dad struggled for the right word, then shrugged. "Less striking."

He thinks I look like a girl. Like a woman.

The waiter bustled back, eyes widening as he saw Dad's hand on mine. "How 'bout some refills for you two?" he asked, smiling.

Before I could stop myself, I wrenched my hand away, hiding it in my lap. Dad looked confused, then angry. He glanced up at the waiter, ready to say something.

"Stop it," I said, not sure which one I was talking to.

"Sorry," the waiter said, his face smoothing back into a professional mask. "Anything else I can get for you?" I shook my head, and he left.

"What the . . . what the *hell*," Dad sputtered as comprehension began to dawn on his face.

"Dad, never mind, please," I said, unable to meet his eyes.

"San Francisco," he mumbled under his breath. Unbelievably, he seemed amused. "Well, I just figured out our next stop."

I had not visited Dad's office in years, not since we moved away from the Bay Area when I was ten. I saw that his name was one of the six on the polished gold plate outside the elevator doors. I looked at him questioningly and he nodded.

"I'm one of the partners here. You knew that." If I had, I'd forgotten. But I nodded. "It's a good thing I had some standing in the firm when all this happened." He shook his head. "It's been a hell of a struggle these last few years."

I looked at Dad closely for the first time since I had come home. He looked older than I remembered, careworn, and like me, too thin.

"I don't begrudge a minute of the time I spent looking for you, Jeff. But I had to put the time in here too, to justify the salary they were giving me. Without that money, the whole operation would have fallen apart."

He wanted something from me, some kind of absolution, I could tell. I shifted, uncomfortable. I didn't have it in me to give.

"No matter what I was doing, even if I was here, talking to someone about estate planning or something, I was always thinking about you." Dad sighed. "God, you were the only thing I was working for, anyway."

I squirmed, picturing Charlie's face, and Brian's, and suddenly, Connie's.

"It's okay, Dad," I said. "You don't have to explain."

"No, I guess I don't," he said, smiling over at me. "I brought you here to get your hair cut. There's a barbershop right here in the building. It's where I go. The barber's a classic. From the old school."

Great. Buzzcut city.

But I smiled back at him. "Okay."

As Dad and I entered the shop, an elderly man with a fringe of white hair around a bald top stood to greet us. He had been reading the *San Francisco Chronicle* and still held the paper in his hands.

"Mr. Hart, good to see you today." The man looked at me closely and his jaw dropped. I read the headline of his paper upside-down: Missing Boy Returns.

"Good morning, Mel. This is my son, Jeff." Dad pushed me forward and I extended my hand automatically. Mel collected himself fast, smiling warmly. Discretion had to come in handy serving a building full of lawyers.

"Jeff, how are you this fine day?" He shook my hand heartily, pumping it once, then nodding me toward a chair. "Your hair looks clean. Just a cut today?"

"That's fine, Mel," Dad answered, coming around to view me critically. "I want it short, above the ears."

Mel deferred to my dad. "Should we leave some fullness on top, Mr. Hart? That's how most of the young boys are wearing it these days."

"All right. Within reason. None of this floppy, hanging-down-over-shaved-sides stuff."

Mel laughed. "You know me better than that, sir. Though I could do that cut, if someone asked for it."

After fifteen minutes, one of my layers of protection was gone. My face was out, exposed for the world to see. My eyes looked huge. My cheekbones stood out like blades. Even my mouth looked fuller. Dad stood up from the second barber chair, where he'd watched the whole operation. After a moment, he smiled.

"Now, that's a nice job, Mel. You're an artist." He took out a twenty and placed it in the barber's hand with a flourish, waving off the change. Mel smiled broadly.

"I'll tell you, Mr. Hart, this is a handsome lad. Even a butcher couldn't go too far wrong with him. And might I say, sir, how pleased I am your son is back where he belongs?"

Dad's smile grew a little strained. "Thank you, Mel. I'm sure I don't need to mention we're trying to keep this as quiet as possible for as long as possible?"

Solemnly, Mel assured him he wouldn't think of breathing a word of our visit to anyone. Once we were outside, I ran a hand over my hair.

"Feels better, doesn't it?" Dad grinned at me, then flicked the ear where I'd worn the diamond ear stud. "That hole will close up on its own, if you leave it alone. I read that somewhere."

I half-listened to Dad, my ear tingling where he had touched it. My attention was focused on a man standing by the elevators, his back to us as he studied the list of names on the directory.

It can't be him. There's no way. . . .

The man was Ray's height, but his posture was

erect, far from Ray's casual slouch. Ray lived in denims and T-shirts; this man wore an expensively cut gray suit. Ray's hair was long, feathered out over his collar; this man's hair was as tightly clipped as mine. The color, though, was the same: black and gray mixed.

I knew it was Ray. I had lived with the man too long, too closely, not to recognize his presence, however he had changed his looks.

He turned around, spotted us and smiled. I froze, dead inside, watching Ray as he walked toward us.

"Excuse me," he said formally, all of his attention on Dad. "I'm looking for the firm of Bowman, Leikus and Harrison. Someone said it was in this building."

Dad shook his head. "No, that's two blocks from here."

Ray chuckled self-deprecatingly. "I'm having a hell of a time finding the place. I wonder if you could . . . "

"Sure," Dad said, after a quick glance at me. "I'll point you in the right direction, anyway." He gestured for Ray to follow him. As they made their way to the lobby doors, Ray looked back, signaling me with his eyes. I could not interpret his message, and I watched him blankly, waiting for whatever it was to happen.

"Bowman, Leikus is two blocks over, to your right," Dad said, pushing one of the heavy glass doors open and leaning halfway out. "See? The redbrick building, past the flag."

"Oh yes. I see it now. Thank you." Ray walked out past Dad without another look back. Dad watched after him for a moment, then shrugged, turning back to me.

"Dave has some more pictures he wants you to look through," he said, walking over. "We're supposed to meet him at the FBI building in a few minutes. It's an easy walk from here."

"I have to go to the bathroom," I said, trying to keep my face steady.

"Sure. Come on, I'll walk you there."

"No," I said. "Just . . . where?"

"Just around the corner from the elevators," he said, pointing. "Are you all right?"

I nodded, walking away quickly. As soon as I was out of his sight I leaned against the wall, trying to catch my breath.

Why why would he be here? Why? It doesn't make any sense he . . .

"Jeff?" Dad was standing in front of me, frowning. "What's wrong?"

"Nothing," I said. "I didn't have to go after all."

He did not look convinced. "You're so pale. What is it? Do you feel sick?"

I plastered a smile on my face. "I'm fine. My stomach's a little upset, that's all."

"Well . . . " Dad hesitated.

"Really," I told him. "I'm okay." My smile faltered when I realized how alone we were in the empty, echoing hallway. "Can we go see Mel again? I forgot to say thanks . . . you know, for the haircut."

Dad was looking at me strangely. "Sure, if you want."

The lobby was empty, and Mel had a sign in his

window announcing he would be back at 1:00 P.M. Ray could have come back into the building. He could be anywhere. . . .

"Dad, can we go up to your office? Mr. Stephens could meet us there, couldn't he?"

He stared at me. "Why?"

"Can you call him and ask if he'll . . . "

"Why would I want to do that?" Dad said. "The FBI building is just a few blocks away. Are you tired, is that it?"

I restrained myself from looking wildly around the lobby. The territory outside the building was uncontrolled. But if Ray caught us outside, at least there would be other people around, and room to run.

"You're right," I told Dad. "We should go over there. Sorry." He watched me for an uncomfortably long moment, then nodded.

Stephens sat waiting for us on a low brick wall that surrounded a fountain in the lobby of the FBI building. He raised his eyebrows at the sight of me. I stopped, self-conscious, remembering my hair.

"That's quite a change," he said.

"We'll have him back to himself in no time," Dad said, but he sounded distracted.

Stephens looked from Dad to me, then back again. I was finding it hard to breathe, knowing what I had to do.

"Well," Stephens said, "have you guys had lunch yet? There's a Mexican place across the street. Jeff can look over the new pictures while we eat."

I folded my arms across my chest, looking down. "I don't need to look at any pictures," I mumbled.

Stephens sighed. "Jeff, this isn't fun for any of us. But it has to be done, you know that."

I looked up at him slowly. He went still, catching something in my expression. "What is it, Jeff?" he said at length.

"I remembered his name," I blurted out, feeling dizzy.

Next to me, Dad stiffened. "You said his name was Ray."

Stephens came forward. "Hang on, Ken. Jeff, sit down for a minute." He gestured back toward the rock wall where he had been sitting.

To my horror I began to cry. I stumbled past Stephens to the wall, sitting down hard, almost missing the ledge. Embarrassed, angry at myself, I rubbed my hands over my face, fighting for control.

"He's been upset about something all morning," Dad told Stephens in a low voice. "I don't know . . . he's hard to reach."

I'm right here, Dad, I wanted to shout. I didn't. I leaned forward, staring at the floor, feeling the light spray of the fountain hitting against my back.

Stephens sat down—not next to me, but in front of me, several feet away, Indian-style on the floor. He looked ridiculous, and if I'd had the energy I would have been insulted at his caution with me. Dad stood a few feet behind him, hands on his hips, looking down.

"What did you remember?" Stephens spoke slowly.

"His last name. Ray's last name. I saw it on an envelope once."

"What is it?"

"Slaight. His name is Ray Slaight. Not S-l-a-t-e. It's spelled S-l-a-i-g-h-t."

"And below that name," Stephens said quietly. "The address on the envelope. Do you remember that?"

"*No.* Just his name. Ray Slaight."

"All right," Stephens said. "We're going to find him."

It's too late for that.

"Raymond Lucas Slaight," Stephens said, glancing down at the yellow legal pad in his hand. "Forty-two years old. He is a lawyer, or was."

Dad nodded. Connie was next to him on the couch, tense, her back perfectly straight. Brian sat on the floor next to her, watching Stephens. Charlie was nearby, curled up in an armchair, her feet drawn up underneath her. She caught my eye as I paced by the window, across the room from the rest of them, and smiled encouragingly at me.

"Jeff," she said softly, patting the arm of the chair, indicating that I should sit there. Everyone turned to stare at me.

"No," I said rudely, looking away from Charlie as a hurt expression crossed her face.

"Slaight worked for a firm in Los Angeles," Stephens continued, looking down at his notes again, then back at Dad. "But he lived in Costa Mesa. Four years ago he was convicted of assault, the only evidence of a criminal record I found. He served four months in the L.A. county jail." For the first time since Stephens had entered the room, I relaxed.

See, Ray may be a criminal, but he's a normal criminal, not . . .

" 'Assault' could mean anything, though," Stephens said. "Sexual attacks against children, particularly boys, are often bargained down to simple assault." He curled his lip as I froze. "The lawyers always say it's to protect the victim. Of course, the one who really benefits is the perpetrator. He goes into jail as a tough guy who beat somebody up, not a pervert who raped a kid."

My face flamed. I glared at Stephens.

Don't talk that way in front of them.

"I'm going down to Southern California tomorrow to see what I can find out," Stephens said.

"While you're gone . . . " Connie said nervously, clutching at Brian's shoulder.

"Don't worry. I have an agent stationed in the lobby."

"That's not necessary," Dad said. "I've got . . . "

Stephens raised his hands. "Don't tell me anything I'll have to officially discourage you against. Look, the agent is just a nice, precautionary measure. The odds are Slaight is long gone. Someone else's headache by now," he added. I held my face expressionless. "What you do have to worry about is if the media finds out where you're staying. At least my guy downstairs can keep them away."

Dad nodded grudgingly. He stood as Stephens did,

reaching out to shake his hand. "All right. Good luck. And thanks."

"Sure," Stephens said. He pointed at me. "Jeff, take care. I'll see you soon." I nodded, wanting to tell him that his trip would be useless, that I wanted him here, yes, *here.*

As Stephens turned to leave, his pager beeped.

"You mind?" he asked, not waiting for Dad's nod as he strode over to the living room phone, which happened to be near me. I backed away, but Stephens ignored me as he quickly punched in the number he read off the pager.

"Who could that be?" Connie said nervously. No one bothered to answer her. I watched Stephens's face.

The person on the other end of the line was doing all the talking, and I could hear the agitation in his voice. My stomach tightened.

It's about me.

"Yeah, he's here," Stephens said shortly. "I'll be right down." He hung up and turned to Dad. "Ken, this has to be fast, so don't argue with me. The agent downstairs has someone in custody resembling Slaight."

"*What?*" Dad said, the color draining out of his face.

Stephens was already shaking his head. "I know you want to be there but you can't. Stay with the family and I'll call you as soon as I can. *Don't leave this room.*" With that, Stephens ran off, slamming the door after him.

Dad watched him go, motionless, one hand on the

back of the couch where Connie sat. She looked up at him, reaching for his hand, her face as pale as his.

"Jeff," Charlie said finally, breaking the silence. "Oh my God. What does he want?"

"Maybe it's not him," Brian said.

"Shut up," Dad barked. "Both of you. No one say anything."

I started counting silently: *one one thousand, two one thousand, three one thousand* . . .

"The hell with this," Dad said suddenly, pulling away from Connie and heading for the door.

"No, Ken," Connie called after him, half rising from the couch, her face stricken.

"Dad, don't," I said, wrapping my arms around my stomach to ease the ache inside. He stopped, looking back at me. "Please don't leave. Please."

He winced as though I had struck him. "I didn't leave," he said, quietly angry. "I didn't leave. You understand that?"

He wasn't making much sense, but I thought I understood him.

Don't blame me for what happened to you.

THE NEXT DAY, STEPHENS DROVE DAD AND ME to the San Francisco county jail, where I was to try to pick Ray out of a lineup. A mob of reporters and cameramen were milling around outside the front entrance to the jail as we passed by on our way to the private parking area. Once they realized who was in Stephens's Volvo, they rushed over, blocking the entrance to the lot, shouting questions and holding microphones out as if we were about to roll the windows down for them. A few cameramen pushed through, shoving their lenses right against the car's windows. The reporters followed, throwing out questions like darts.

"Jeff, are you happy to be home?"

"Is your kidnapper inside?"

"Did he molest you, Jeff?"

"Jeff, how does it feel to be back?"

I closed my ears to them, amazed by the fuss and scared too. Dad reached back over the seat and patted my head roughly.

"Don't worry about them," he said. "Don't worry about anything."

The reporters fell back only slightly as Stephens pulled forward by inches.

"Can't you do something?" Dad snarled, reaching between Stephens's arms to blast the horn.

"Hey, that won't help," Stephens said. But the reporters moved back enough then for him to slide the Volvo in past the gate.

"Is he in there?" I asked quietly, after Stephens piloted the car into a space near the side entrance of the jail.

"That's for you to tell us," Stephens said carefully. "After you see the lineup."

I promised him I would never do this.

When Dad turned around again, I realized I had spoken out loud.

"It doesn't matter what you promised him." Dad's eyes were fierce.

The building was dingy inside, the walls painted a dull green, a faint chemical odor hanging over the hallways. I avoided the eyes of the men and women in uniform, but several of them stopped anyway to shake my hand.

"Why do they know me?" I asked Stephens.

He smiled. "You don't realize yet what a concerted effort there was to find you."

The lineup room was dimly lit and cluttered with folding chairs. One wall was blocked off by olive green curtains. A short, heavy female officer shook hands with Stephens, Dad and me. Two men in suits stood against the back wall. They did not introduce themselves.

"Jeff, I'm going to open these drapes," the officer said, meeting my eyes squarely. "You'll see five men standing in a lineup. They can't see you. Take your time, and look carefully at each man."

Dad pushed me gently toward the curtained window. I shivered, gooseflesh breaking out on my arms.

"They can't see you. They can't get at you," he whispered. I felt the dusty folds of the drapes against my nose, and for a moment I couldn't breathe.

"Not so close, please." Dad let me go immediately, stepping away. "No," I said, turning to him. "Just . . . I don't want to be that close to the window."

"Of course." Dad hesitated. "He can do this sitting down, can't he?"

"Sure," the officer said, gesturing back to the rows of folding chairs.

"Jeff, I'll get you a chair and you can sit."

"I don't need a chair, Dad!"

Everyone was silent until the officer cleared her throat.

"I'm going to open the curtain now, all right?" She pulled at some hidden cords. I did not look up.

"Jeff," Dad said softly.

"I can't. I'm sorry, but I can't."

Stephens stood behind me now.

"C'mon, kid," he whispered. "Take a look at these guys. Get it over with."

I walked away from him, toward the window.

All of the men in the lineup had dark hair and pale

skin. All stood about six feet tall. The third man was clearly Ray—a different Ray than the one I had known, but Ray nonetheless. This Ray was clean-shaven and stood straight and proud and sported a military haircut like mine. To my horror, he was looking right at me.

From a distance, I heard Dad say, "Jesus Christ." I put my hands up to the glass and stared. Ray stared back at me boldly, and my focus narrowed down to his eyes.

I turned to Stephens. "She said he couldn't see me." I sounded calm, no indication of what was going on inside me.

"He can't," Stephens said. "No one in that room can see in here. It's impossible. Those men are looking at their own reflections in a mirror."

"He can see me. He's looking at me now."

"Jeff, you have to say the number. Do you see the man who kidnapped you?"

"The third one. From the left. That's Ray."

"Are you sure?"

I began to tremble uncontrollably. "Yes."

"Fine," Stephens said briskly.

"Where's the bathroom?" I managed to choke out, breaking for the door.

"It's down the hallway to your right," the officer called after me.

I found the men's restroom with no trouble. But once I was there, I could do nothing. I tasted vomit at the back of my throat, caught in a lump, but it wouldn't move. Leaning back against the tile wall, I wrapped my arms around my stomach. The bathroom door opened and I straightened up quickly. It was Dad.

"How are you feeling? Dumb question, I know." He came closer and I could see that his eyes were moist. "Did you throw up?"

"No." I hid my face in my hands for a moment.

Dad sighed and turned on the water. He washed his hands, then his face, then turned back to me.

"Dave said the man you identified is Slaight. If I had a gun, I'd kill him right now."

"Don't do that," I said distantly.

"Jeff, I'm not angry with you." I looked up at him slowly. "But I need you to tell me something. Is Ray Slaight the same man who asked me for directions yesterday?"

I closed my eyes. "Yes. I'm sorry, Dad. I'm . . . sorry."

"Okay," he said softly, "you're under a tremendous strain, I know. But why didn't you say something? My God."

"I couldn't tell you then."

"Why?" Dad demanded. I flinched at his tone. "I'm not trying to scare you . . . "

"You're not scaring me."

"Don't you see, if I'd known I could have *done* something. Why didn't you give me the chance to do right by you this time?"

"Does it matter now? We're here, he's there—"

"Of course it matters!" Dad snapped. "Why didn't you tell me it was him?"

"I was scared, all right? He's . . . " I fumbled for the right word. "Ray is crazy."

"I can be crazy too when it comes to defending my son," Dad said, his voice passionate.

I looked away, embarrassed. "Can we go now?"

Dad turned the water on again and moistened a paper towel.

"Wash your face," he said, handing it to me.

I obeyed him, feeling the thin, damp paper turning warm against my skin. I crumpled the paper into a soggy ball, then tossed it into a wall-mounted waste-can. Dad handed me a second towel to dry off.

"Let's go find Dave," he said when I was done.

Stephens led us to an interview room that was small and icily air-conditioned. A woman sat in the corner with a typewriter-like device and a laptop computer. A tape recorder was built into the wall over the white metal table where Stephens indicated we should sit.

Without preliminaries, Dad said, "When I took Jeff to get his hair cut in my building yesterday, Slaight was there. I don't know if he followed us, or knew where I worked and got lucky, or—"

"How did that happen, Jeff?" Stephens asked, his eyes intense. I shrugged. "Did you have an arrangement to meet him there?"

My detachment vanished in an instant. "*What?* No!" I turned to Dad. "You don't think that, do you?"

He hesitated just a second too long. "No. Of course not."

"Ray and I are not a team, okay?" I glared at Stephens. "How can you say that?" He didn't answer. "I wouldn't walk Dad into an ambush."

"Is that what it was, an ambush? Was Slaight armed, do you think?"

I relaxed a little. "Probably," I mumbled. "He had guns. And knives."

"Did he use them on you?" Stephens asked.

"No," I flared at him. "I'm here, aren't I?"

"I mean, did he threaten you with weapons?"

I looked from Stephens to Dad, to the young black stenographer, who looked away quickly when I met her eyes.

"He held a knife on me when he forced me into his van," I said flatly.

"This is when he kidnapped you?" I nodded. "Okay, tell us about it."

I looked straight at Stephens, avoiding Dad's eyes. "This is all I'm going to say. I'll tell you how he kidnapped me. That's it." Stephens remained expressionless. I waited for his agreement.

"Go on," he said finally.

"Ray came up behind me," I said. "That day. I didn't hear him. He held a knife to my throat. He cut me a little." I was back in that hot afternoon, feeling moisture on my neck, the cut stinging as sweat mingled with blood. "He walked me to his van, pushed me inside, and that was it."

"What happened next? Where did he take you?"

I shook my head. "He kidnapped me," I said. "That's a crime, isn't it?"

"Yes, that's a crime," Stephens said.

"So what more do you need? Ray kidnapped me. He kept me with him a long time and he made sure I couldn't leave. . . . " I stopped, flushing.

"How did he make sure you couldn't leave?" Stephens's voice was quiet. "Did he abuse you? Did he physically abuse you?"

I clenched my hands into fists, shaking my head over and over again. Finally I answered him. "No. I told you no."

"Jeff has a point," Dad said, clearing his throat. "You've got Slaight cold on kidnapping. That's enough for now, isn't it? Come on, this has been one hell of a day."

Stephens sighed. "Ken, he's got to—"

"No," Dad said. "Not now. Let him alone."

Stephens agreed to put off the rest of my "interrogation" until he had a chance to question Ray extensively and investigate his background. Though the relief came to me like air, I knew the reprieve was a brief one: Stephens would be back. All I could count on to protect me from his insinuations was Ray's instinct for self-preservation, and I wondered how strong that was. I pictured him again in the lineup: no attempt to blend in, the heavy stare into the mirror, the half smile on his face.

That expression was all I saw the entire three hour drive back to Wayne. I faked sleep to avoid questions, my eyes shut, my head lolling against the window. But no one was talking.

It was after ten when we arrived. I hurried up to my room, eager to be alone. But once I was there I began to feel scared again. All I could think about was Ray and how I had betrayed him. He would find a way to make me pay for that, I knew. I sat on the bed, wide awake, wondering how I was going to get through the night.

"Jeff?" Charlotte said, leaning into the room. "You

want to play Monopoly with me and Brian?" I hesitated. "Come on. Dad said he didn't mind if we stay up for a while."

"Okay," I said.

We met Dad in the hallway. "You're going to play a game downstairs?" he asked. I nodded. "Good. But don't make it too late. I want you up early tomorrow to run some errands with me."

"Okay, Dad," I promised. He gathered me to him, hugging me hard, releasing me quickly. It was over before I could react and then Dad retreated to his bedroom. I looked up slowly and caught Charlie's cynical expression as she waited for me to join her on the stairs.

"You're more popular than me," she said dryly.

"I'm sorry" was all I could think to say.

"Forget it." She shrugged and walked down the stairs ahead of me.

Brian had already set up the Monopoly board on the living room floor. He looked up at me eagerly. "Hi, Jeff. You want to be real estate agent? I'm banker."

"Nah, let Charlie do it if she wants," I said, sitting down across from him. He looked so forlorn, I added, "Okay, I'll do it. Unless . . . Charlie?"

"I can live without it," she said sarcastically.

I had that "new kid" feeling, a sort of clammy awkwardness and hyperconsciousness of every move I made. In the few days I had been home—less than a week, I realized suddenly—I had barely spoken to either of them.

"Hey, Brian," I tried, setting the Monopoly real estate cards into neat rows on the floor, "how come I had to get this buzzcut, and you get to keep yours long?" Brian's hair was collar length, and he kept flipping it back out of his eyes. Charlie shot me a look. Her message was clear.

Because Dad couldn't care less what Brian's hair looks like, dummy. Remember?

Brian grinned. "I like my hair long. Most of the guys wear it this way. Vin Perini does."

"He does? Well, he always did." I finished setting up the cards. "Come on," I said, assuming the leadership role I had once held. "Let's roll to see who goes first."

Charlie picked up the dice and rolled a six. Brian moved closer to me, not watching the board. His closeness made me uncomfortable but I stayed where I was.

"Vin's in the paper a lot," Brian said. "He's the quarterback for the varsity football team. He was last year too, and he was only a sophomore then. He plays varsity baseball too."

"You know a lot about him," I said casually, as if I didn't care.

"You should ask Charlie. She's the real expert." Brian giggled.

Charlie blushed. "Vin says 'hi' to me at school and I work with him at the stables sometimes. That's it!" She looked at me shyly. "He really is a nice guy, though. He came up to me the first day of school and said if I needed anything, I should just ask him. Wasn't that nice?"

"Wasn't that *nice*," Brian simpered, clasping his hands in front of his chest.

"Shut up, Brian. I don't like him that way. Anyway, he goes out with Jana Hunter. She's so phony. Boys have no taste."

Brian sighed extravagantly. "Jana Hunter is *so* pretty, Jeff."

"Charlie's pretty too," I said. She looked at me quickly, skeptical.

"Her?" Brian gasped, then laughed.

"Yeah, we have a pretty sister," I said.

"Yeah, right," Charlie said, hunching her shoulders. But now she was smiling.

"It's your turn to roll the dice, Brian," I told him.

The game became so absorbing I lost track of time, until my stomach reminded me I had to eat something. "You guys want some food?" I asked, still feeling constrained about going into the kitchen and just taking what I wanted.

"There's probably still some chocolate chip cookies," Charlie said. "They might be stale."

"That's okay," I said, my stomach growling. "Let's eat 'em anyway."

The three of us sat cross-legged on the floor picking cookies off a platter, sipping milk from heavy crystal drinking glasses.

"Dad doesn't like us to eat in the living room," Brian whispered.

"Screw him," Charlie said quietly. Brian looked at her, stricken. "Lighten up, Bri! I'm kidding."

"You shouldn't talk about him that way," he said, staring at the floor.

Charlie and I exchanged glances.

"Brian . . . " she started, then softened her tone. "Sorry, okay?"

"Okay," he said, brightening. "What about Christmas?" he demanded.

"Christmas?" I asked. "When is it?"

"Two days," Charlie said automatically. "They'll do something, probably. Connie usually has to drag Dad into it. Not this year, though." I looked at her quickly, but she just smiled.

"Jeff, that guy you were with . . . " Brian spoke hesitantly.

I froze.

"Did he give you presents? At Christmas, I mean."

"Brian . . . " Charlie said softly, shaking her head.

"You were gone *two* Christmases," Brian said, ignoring her. I heard something like awe in his voice.

I looked at his stupid, innocent face, avid with curiosity, and hated him a little. Charlie was more subdued, but she watched me too, leaning forward, her legs drawn up in front of her, arms wrapped around her knees.

I press my body hard against the stucco wall, face first, my arms outstretched, running my fingers up and down the ridged surface, working to convince myself that I am alive in this darkness that has gone on for . . . two days? Five? A week? More?

I hear the first door opening. My heart pounding in

excitement and terror, I scramble across the room. When the second door opens I am sitting on the bed, facing him, hands folded in my lap, my back against the wall, the way he has told me to wait for him.

The light spilling in from the passageway doesn't hit my face but it is light and it burns my eyes. I put my head down, covering my eyes with the heels of both hands, ready for him to pull the cord to the overhead light, the light he used to disable each time he left me, the one he trusts now I will not touch.

This time is different. He grabs my hands away from my eyes and pulls me off the bed.

"Come on," he says. "You're going out." He pulls a black silk bandanna out of his pocket, tying it tightly around my head.

He leads me, none too gently, through the garage. I slip a little when I step into a patch of greasy fluid, and he drags me a few steps. I regain my footing and I am outside for the first time since the day he took me.

I stop, taking in lungfuls of the fresh, icy air, my ears perked to listen for any sounds, any life beyond Ray. I hear nothing, and he yanks my arm hard to get me moving.

My feet skip over sharp pebbles, and I step glancingly on a thorn. I cry out and he releases me for a second to slap my face. "Sorry," I tell him, and then we are on flat stone—concrete by the feel of it. The relief is immense.

He pushes a door open and we are in another building. We walk over cool tile onto a bare wooden floor, *then he pushes me into another room, catching me as I nearly trip over a throw rug. He steadies me, then pulls off the blindfold.*

The room is small, square and sparsely furnished. It is a living room, with a fireplace that looks unused and no pictures on the walls. Dusty-looking floor-length beige curtains shield the room's one window. A tall lamp set on an end table provides the only light.

There is a Christmas tree in one corner, a few red and green ornaments hanging off it. Brightly wrapped packages are scattered underneath on the bare floor. I say nothing, not sure what Ray wants me to do. He points toward the tree. I am very aware of his muscular arm outstretched inches from my head.

"You like it?" His voice is deceptively casual.

"The tree?" I ask, flinching in advance. But Ray is in a good mood, and he laughs, cuffing me lightly on the back of the head.

"The tree, the presents, all of it. It's Christmas, you jerk."

"Christmas?" I repeat. My voice is dull, stunned.

"You're staying with me tonight," he tells me. I barely hear him.

Christmas. I have been with him eight months.

Charlie and Brian came back into focus, still watching me.

"Ray and I had great Christmases," I told them, feeling mean.

"Really?" Brian asked. "What did you do?"

"Brian." Charlie looked uncomfortable. "You don't

have to say anything, Jeff. Let's just play Monopoly, okay?"

"No," Brian said insistently. "He doesn't mind talking about this, right, Jeff?"

"You know what Dad said," Charlie warned, then looked at me quickly, covering her mouth with one hand.

"Since when do you care what Dad says?" Brian asked, keeping his voice down.

"What did Dad say?" I asked Charlie.

"Well . . . " she said slowly. "Nothing really. Just that we should leave you alone and not bother you. You know, especially about what happened."

I nodded, trembling inside, thinking of the four of them sitting around discussing me and the best way to handle my problems.

"You don't mind talking about it, do you?" Brian asked.

The silence that followed grew tense as I didn't answer. Charlie watched me anxiously. Finally I smiled. "No. Go ahead. What do you want to know?"

"Really?" Brian said. "I can ask you anything?"

Charlie groaned. "Brian . . . "

"I'm not talking to you," he said, turning on her fiercely.

"What do you want to know?" I repeated.

"Well . . . " Brian was suddenly shy. "Was he nice to you? That man?"

"Sure," I said, smiling. "He was a little extreme, but—"

"What do you mean 'extreme'?" Brian asked.

"Would you just leave him alone?" Charlie said.

"Shut up!" he snarled, turning back to me. "So he treated you okay?"

"Ray was great to me," I said. "We played games together. Not like Monopoly though. You want me to show you one?" Brian nodded.

"That's okay, you don't have to show us," Charlie said, drawing back.

"Don't worry, Charlie," I said. "It's not a dirty one."

She looked shocked. "I didn't mean that," she protested. "I wouldn't—"

"Hey, Brian," I said. "You remember 'Staredown'?"

"Sure."

"Well, Ray used to play that with me a lot. He played it different than we used to, though. You want me to show you?"

"Yeah!"

"Jeff . . . " Charlie tried again. I ignored her.

"Okay, go stand against the wall." Brian leapt up and ran over to the wall next to the fireplace. "Stand back as far as you can," I said. "Don't leave any space behind you."

"Okay," Brian called. "I'm ready."

I walked toward him slowly, my stomach churning in a mix of fear, disgust and, I recognized, excitement. Charlie tried to catch my arm and I shook her off. I didn't stop until I was directly in front of Brian. I leaned down to him, so close our noses almost touched. Brian tried to back up but he had nowhere to go.

"Jeff, stop it," Charlie said more insistently, pushing at my shoulder.

My eyes never leaving Brian's, I shoved her hard, feeling a thrill at her softness yielding to my force.

"Okay," I said, "Let's go. The first one to break the stare gets slapped."

"That's not how you play," Brian protested weakly, a nervous smile flickering across his lips.

I nodded. "Right. But see, that's how *Ray* plays. If you break the stare, you get slapped. You get slapped every time you look away from him, so the only way to win is to never look away. . . . "

Brian was crying now, cringing, his arms trembling as he tried to keep them by his sides to avoid touching me. The tension drained out of me and I felt weak again, weak and so disgusted with myself I wanted to die.

"Sorry," I said, stepping away from him, no idea where to go next. I did not want to return upstairs so soon and risk an encounter with Dad. I considered trying to sleep in the guest room, but I did not think Connie had cleaned it since Stephens had slept there. I pictured myself lying on his sweaty, rumpled sheets and a shudder ran through me.

I sat down on the couch, staring into space.

"Jeff." Brian stood in front of me, still crying. "I'm sorry, I shouldn't have asked."

Charlie stood next to him. "What can we do, is there anything?" She sounded as young and helpless as Brian.

I shook my head slowly, then managed to say, "Leave me alone." I heard my brother blaming himself and my sister telling him to be quiet. "One thing," I choked out, repeating myself until they stopped arguing. "Don't tell Dad."

"Hey, kiddo," Dad said, shaking me gently awake. I sat up, rubbing my eyes, aware suddenly that something was wrong.

"What?" I asked, choking on the word.

"Hey, relax." Dad laughed a little, but his eyes were sad. "Nothing too awful. The press is outside." I just looked at him. "It's nothing like it was in San Francisco. But they're here, they want to see you, and I think we should just get it over with."

"Talk to them, you mean?"

Dad nodded.

"I don't want to," I said, finally awake.

"I know. But they're not going away until they get a clear shot of you, and . . . " He sighed. "It's reality. So let's give them one look, and then go on about our business. All right?"

"Yeah, whatever," I muttered.

"Okay then. Meet you downstairs."

Though we could have left the house through the attached garage, Dad steered me out the front door instead, indicating by pressure that I should stop at the top of the porch steps. I stepped forward another inch, losing Dad's hand off my shoulder, looking out at them.

Four vans, each with television call letters painted on their sides, were parked along the sidewalk outside our lawn. Four ill-matched sets of people stood near the vans, conferring with each other: well-dressed reporters and their work-suited camera operators. Conspicuously apart from this group was a handful of men and women carrying notepads, tape recorders and their own cameras.

"There he is," one of the plainly dressed reporters said, sounding more conversational than excited, and the entire group headed for me.

"There's a lot of them," I said flatly, scared. Dad squeezed my shoulder again and this time I deliberately shook him off.

"A lot of them," Dad agreed quietly. "But it's all right. I'll handle it."

With that he stepped alongside me, smiling out at everyone, a smile so phony I was surprised to see many of them smile back.

"Mr. Hart, how do you feel about all this?" a blond woman asked. At eight in the morning, she was wearing a cocktail dress and high heels.

"We feel great, of course, Cheryl," Dad said. I looked at him sideways. Cheryl?

"Our boy is home," Dad continued, smiling at Cheryl, then past her. "We couldn't be happier." The television reporters nodded sympathetically while the print reporters scribbled into their notebooks, frowning.

"Are you glad the guy is in custody?" a young, athletic-looking man asked, another of the TV reporters.

"Sure," Dad said, still smiling, his voice tightening just a little. "For everyone's sake. Let's not talk about him here."

"Jeff!" someone said quietly in the lull that followed. I saw an earnest-looking woman with short gray hair standing on the edge of the print reporters' circle. She smiled at me, so genuinely I smiled back. "What's the next step for you?" she asked.

"I don't know." I looked at Dad uncertainly. "School, I guess."

He nodded, clapping his hands once. "Well, folks, we've got errands to run, so—"

"Jeff, did the guy molest you?" I looked down to the speaker: a pudgy young man dressed in wrinkled chinos and a stained white polo shirt. He waited patiently for my answer, unimpressed by my silence.

Dad had a grip on my shoulder again. "Thanks, everyone." With that he guided me down the steps and through the reporters, pointing the remote-control door opener in the general direction of the garage.

Dad waited a moment before we pulled out, taking a deep breath, staring down at his hands. Then he backed out slowly, putting on another smile. He rolled down the window as the reporters took their time stepping out of his way.

"Take care now," he called, raising his hand briefly. Most of the reporters smiled back to him or nodded, though my last interrogator stood glumly in the middle of the road, staring after us.

"Bastards," Dad hissed as we drove around the corner.

Chilled by the encounter, unsettled, I hit what seemed to be the safest point. "It seemed like you knew them."

"I do," Dad said. "Some of them. I put in my time with the press." He looked over at me. "They're not all bad, but . . . " He shook his head. "All right, we've done that. So."

I was silent as we turned onto Wayne's main street. Dad glanced at me again.

"That should hold them for a while. But if anything happens with Slaight, anything with the case, they'll be back."

"Okay, okay," I muttered, folding my arms across my chest, looking down.

"I might not be here to protect you then." Dad sounded like he was talking to himself. "I have to get back to work eventually."

Suddenly, unaccountably furious with him, I lashed out. "Hey, don't worry about it. You don't have to *protect* me from anything. He's in jail, isn't he?"

We were both quiet after that. Then Dad let out his breath in a harsh sigh, his fingers tightening on the steering wheel.

"Sorry," I said quickly. "I shouldn't have said that."

He held up a hand without looking at me. "It's all right."

Dad drove another mile or so to a huge shopping center that had been a cow pasture the last time I'd seen it.

"Okay!" he said briskly once we were in the store. "I'll need your help here. Connie's list is two pages long."

I shuffled along behind him, feeling as out of place as if we'd landed on the moon. We walked through an enormous archway into the store, where Dad nodded toward the carts. He handed me one page of the list.

"Let's each take a cart. You stay near me and look for the things on your list. You see anything you want for yourself, toss it in." He caught my eyes and tried to smile. "We've got to get you back to your fighting weight."

I let Dad lead me through the store. It was a tedious, deliberate process, as I didn't know where anything was and he constantly had to come back and check my list. Finally he just took it from me and used my cart as backup. I wanted to get some kind of food for myself to please him, but I didn't see anything that appealed to me. Finally I grabbed a box of Sugar Pops and some chocolate chip ice cream, food I had enjoyed as a child.

I kept my eyes down, but I sensed a few people staring at me, and I thought I heard some whispers. I ignored them, telling myself I was imagining things. But once Dad and I reached the checkout counter, the game was up. The thin, dark-haired woman checking the groceries was Marie Perini. Vin's mother.

"Oh my God! Is that *you?* Oh Geez! Jeff Hart!"

"Hi, Marie," I said. She ran out from behind the counter, pushed past Dad, and grabbed me. I could see from Dad's face that he was seriously pissed and about to move her off, but I signaled him it was all right. She rocked me side to side, reaching up to kiss my cheek.

"You're so tall . . . and handsome! Oh, you grew up. You back in town permanent now?"

I shrugged, bewildered by the question.

"Vinny's going to be so excited! He's missed you so much, never stopped talking about you." Marie clasped me tighter and I smelled her perfume and powder.

"It's good to see you," I said, detaching myself gently. "How are you?"

Marie let me go, patting my cheek. "I'm fine, honey, the question is, how are *you?*"

"I'm okay."

"Out shopping with Dad, huh?" she said, punching him lightly on the arm. He did not look happy.

"We're in a hurry, Mrs. Perini," he told her, gesturing toward the groceries.

Marie nodded. "Of course, don't mind me." She scurried back behind the counter and began dragging items over the scanner, talking all the while. "You are coming over to see Vinny, aren't you?"

When I didn't answer, she shook a loaf of bread at me. "Don't be shy. You *are,* or we'll come get you."

Her face tightened and she addressed Dad. "Mr. Hart, if it was me, I would have killed the bastard."

My face reddening, I moved past Dad to where the groceries were piling up. A plastic sack was already set up in a holder at the end of the counter, and I began grabbing items at random and tossing them in the bag.

"Oh no, honey, don't you get those," Marie said. "I'll call someone. Andy!" she screeched over an intercom. Dad winced, and the misery was complete. I recognized the bag boy right away: my grade school enemy Andy Keller. Though he'd grown into a giant, Andy's baby face and wiry blond hair were unmistakable.

"Hey," he said in a monotone. I nodded to him.

Andy and Vin had been best friends when I arrived on the scene in fifth grade. Then, like that, it was Vin and me, and Andy was left out. He had only sneered at Vin's attempts to include him, and finally Vin had shrugged him off. Andy had made it clear then that he hated me, but at the time, I didn't much care. I was becoming Mr. Sports Hero, and Andy was just a mean fat guy hanging on at the edges of the jocks' circle.

It was amazing how little any of that mattered now. Sixteen-year-old Andy stood before me, still fat, but muscular too, immensely tall, carrying himself with a physical confidence I did not remember. Suddenly I was sure that Andy had become a major success as a high school athlete, and that he and Vin were friends again.

He looked me over, curious, then tilted his head back. "Where you been?" I shrugged, looking down.

Andy grunted. Then, with a skill that put my fumblings to shame, he began plucking the groceries up three at a time, packing them neatly into paper bags he lined up along the counter.

Marie, who'd watched our reunion open-mouthed, shook her head and leaned over the counter toward Dad. "It's a crime," she said, lowering her voice without dropping the volume. "It's just a crime. These faggots that prey on our kids, they should be strung up, electrocuted, *tortured* like they torture. I told my boys if some pervert ever comes up to them—"

"Mrs. Perini, check the goddamn groceries." Dad's voice was ice-cold. Marie drew back, glaring at him.

"Fine!" she said, calling out the total, then practically grabbing the check from his hand. Andy stood by the loaded carts, tapping one foot. I knew my face was bright red.

Dad refused Andy's offer to take the groceries out for us. After we had unloaded them, Dad took the carts back while I waited inside the Jeep.

"I'm sorry," Dad said when he returned. "Obviously, I don't do much of the shopping or I never would have gone there. Did you know that kid from school?"

"Yeah," I mumbled. "Andy Keller. Dad, can I ask you something?"

"Of course."

"What she was saying in there . . . " I paused. "And the reporter. Is that what everyone thinks?"

Dad waited a long time before he answered. "That you were molested? Probably." He started up the Jeep but kept it in park for a moment. Then he sighed, and, looking behind him, backed out of the spot.

I waited for him to say more, edgier than I had been since the night I came home. But we were out of the shopping center, headed up to the highway back to town, before Dad spoke again.

"When a child is kidnapped," he said, sounding as though he were weighing out every word, "like you were, the natural assumption is that there's a sexual motive behind it. I knew that from the start, and Dave only confirmed it."

I squirmed. "Yeah? Well, who's *Dave?* And what do you mean 'natural'? There's nothing *natural* about it." I stared down at my hands, curling my toes in embarrassment.

"Jeff . . . " Dad's voice was gentle. It was the start of something I did not want to face. Could not face.

"No!" I said, turning to him for an instant, then looking away fast out the passenger-side window. "It's not true, anyway. It's not true, okay?"

"Okay," Dad said soothingly, placating me.

I turned to him again. "It's not true," I said, working to control my voice. "But if that's what everyone thinks, then what's the point?"

"What do you mean 'what's the point'?" he said, sharp now.

"I mean," I plowed ahead. "I'm supposed to walk around this town, *school,* with everyone thinking I'm a faggot?"

"Don't use that word," Dad said angrily. "Mrs.

Perini was talking trash. I don't want you to waste your time listening to people like that."

I took a deep breath. "Is that what you think about me too?"

"What?" he asked me too quickly. He knew.

"You think I'm a . . . whatever you want me to call it." I saw Dad's knuckles go white on the steering wheel. "Never mind," I said, looking away. We drove in silence for a few minutes until I noticed we weren't heading toward home.

"Where are we going?"

"To pick out a Christmas tree," Dad said with forced cheer.

"Dad . . . " I started.

He glanced over at me, smiling. "Look, I feel the same way. But Connie likes to do the Christmas thing. She wants to do something this year, even though we really only have today and tomorrow." I shrugged. "I've already had my Christmas," he added, his voice thick with emotion.

Feeling utterly cold, I said nothing, staring out the window as we passed the shopping center where Dad used to take us for pizza, the park where I had played Little League baseball for three years, the creek where Vin, Charlie and I had thought we'd found gold once.

Dad flipped on his turn signal and turned into the fairgrounds lot.

"*Here?*" I said, cringing. The last person I wanted to see was Vin. I couldn't remember what hours Connie had said he worked.

Though I made no move for the door, Dad caught my arm. "Jeff. Before we go in—"

"Why are we here?" I said suspiciously.

Dad looked confused for a moment. "Oh!" he said, releasing my arm. "There's a Christmas tree lot here where we usually go."

Where we usually go. Jeff's gone, and life goes on.

"Look," Dad said abruptly. "What we were talking about before, I don't want to let it drop." He waited until I looked at him. "The 'faggot' stuff. No one with any class is going to lay that on you. I don't want you thinking about yourself that way."

"Who says I do?" I challenged him, sounding stronger than I felt.

Dad, so strong and confident and maddeningly *right* all the time, looked helpless. "Jeff . . . "

"Don't," I warned. He sighed, then nodded.

"Okay. Let's go buy a Christmas tree."

"CHARLIE, WHEN DOES SECOND SEMESTER START?"
Dad asked, dishing himself a serving of salad, then passing the bowl to Brian. He had prepared Christmas dinner himself: lasagna, salad and garlic bread. Considering Connie's stunned and pleased reaction, I figured it wasn't something he did very often.

"Three weeks," Charlie said, glancing at me.

Connie laughed a little. "Ken, do you really think he's ready for that?"

"What's the alternative?" Dad said, spearing a tomato and finishing it off in three quick bites. "Trial preparation can take months. Jeff can't sit out the rest of the year. He's missed too much school already."

"He could go on independent study," Charlie said, pushing her hair back. "Sherry's sister does that. She meets with a teacher once a week and does her work at home."

"That's sounds more like me, Dad," I said, thinking of Andy's dead-eyed stare. "If I could do that—"

"No," Dad said firmly. "I want you back into the normal life of a sixteen-year-old boy. That means full-time school and sports activities." Charlie laughed a little, an "a-ha" kind of laugh. "Charlotte, do you have something you want to say?"

She leaned back in her chair. "Yes, if you want me to be honest. Otherwise I can go to my room."

"Say it." Dad's voice was cold.

"This is all about getting Jeff into baseball again, isn't it?" Dad's eyes narrowed. "What if he doesn't care about being a jock anymore?"

"That's his business, not yours," Dad said.

Charlie leaned forward, raising her hands. "Exactly! So why are you pushing him?"

"Dad," I said quickly, "I guess I should go back to school, but I don't know if I can. I mean, I didn't even finish eighth grade. And sports!" I tried to laugh. "I'm totally out of shape. My arm . . . I haven't thrown a ball—"

"All of that is fixable with hard work. I can tutor you, and Connie's a teacher. As for sports, you've always been a natural. The point is, you need to start working on something positive. Connie, how many more days before vacation ends?"

"A week and a day," she said quietly.

"Okay," Dad said. "So everyone goes back to school in just about a week. I'll have to be back at work soon myself. Jeff, I don't want you sitting here by yourself all day."

"Dad, I'll be fine, really."

"I know you will," he said, too quickly. "It's simply better for you to be busy, working toward some kind of goal, something that has nothing to do with the trial."

"Is that guy still in jail?" Brian asked. No one answered him. "Dad," he said, "that guy, is he still—"

"Yes, Brian, I heard you. Yes, he is. You remember what we talked about?" Dad stared at Brian for a moment until he nodded.

The next few minutes passed in heavy silence.

"This is excellent, Ken," Connie said finally, holding up a forkful of lasagna. "Thank God one of us can cook."

Dad smiled at her. "Glad you like it," he said, taking another quick bite of salad.

The phone rang and Dad tensed again. Connie laid a hand on his arm.

"It's probably just Dave," she murmured.

"Too early for that," Dad said, flicking his eyes over me. Stephens called every night around eight to give Dad an update on the case. I never asked what Stephens was saying and Dad didn't volunteer.

Dad walked into the kitchen and grabbed the cordless phone off the counter. I could see him through the doorway and I waited, tense.

"Hello? Who is this?" he asked angrily. "Oh. Sure. How are you?" He sounded much more relaxed. "I'm not sure . . . yes, okay. Just a minute."

Dad came back into the dining room carrying the phone.

"Jeff, it's Vin Perini. He wants to say hello to you."
No. No way.

I stared at Dad, shaking my head. He nodded back at me in a way I could not refuse. "Take the phone. You can talk in the living room."

I took the phone from him and walked into the living room like a zombie. I waited until I was as far away from the dining room as possible before I spoke.

"Hi," I said in a monotone.

"Jeff?" The voice was heavy and deep, much deeper than Vin's. I panicked for a second, looking around for Dad. But the voice was not Ray's either.

He grew up, stupid. Just like Andy. Just like you would have.

"Jeff?"

"Hi," I said again, feeling dumb. But what the hell could I say to him?

"Um, yeah," Vin said. "I don't know if this is a good time to call or not, but I wanted to get in touch. My mom said she saw you in the store the other day. Andy too. I was going to call then, but . . . listen, tell me if this isn't a good time for you."

Vin already sounded like he wanted to hang up. I didn't blame him.

"Sorry," I said awkwardly. "I guess I just don't know what to say."

Vin laughed, sounding relieved. "Yeah, I don't either. Just . . . I'm glad you're back, man. I missed you. I almost went crazy from missing you."

My face reddened. God, how could he say that? Didn't he realize how it sounded?

"Jeff?" Vin said again.

"I'm here."

"Well, listen, you want to get together or something? I could go over there or you could—"

"Now?" I felt panicked again.

"Well, no, not *right* now. It's Christmas. But how about tomorrow? We could play basketball at the high school, if you want, or whatever you want to do."

I closed my eyes, in such pain I did not trust myself to speak. I hit the disconnect button, tossed the phone on the couch, and headed for my room. I lay there in the dark, curled on my side, the door open so I could focus on the light coming in from the hallway.

The phone rang again and I could feel myself blushing, even here, alone in my room.

Dad appeared in the doorway. "Jeff?" he said. "Did you hang up on Vin?"

I rolled onto my back, pressing the heels of my hands against my eyes. "Yes," I mumbled.

"Why?" he said, sitting on the edge of my bed. I sat up quickly, edging away from him. "Jeff?" Dad sounded bewildered.

"I don't want to talk to him."

"But why?" Dad asked. "He's a good kid. He's been a good friend."

"This isn't about what kind of . . . *friend* Vin is," I spat, then looked away, afraid to show Dad that much of my anger.

"Are you embarrassed to talk with him?" Dad asked.

I sat back, bracing myself against the headboard. "Why should I be embarrassed?"

"I don't know. You're acting like you are. That's why I asked."

"Dad, I can't . . . " I started, then broke off.

"Can't what?" he asked, so tenderly tears filled my eyes. I bit down hard on my tongue to stop them. I was not going to cry in front of him again.

"I'm . . . oh, I'm a freak," I told him, hitting my arm hard back against the headboard, wincing as I cracked my elbow. "Leave me alone, please." I was begging now, my pride gone.

"No," Dad said slowly. "I won't leave you alone. I know how hard this is for you. If I could go through it instead of you, I would. But I can't do that, Jeff, and you're just going to have to make your way back into normal life again. Picking up your friendship with Vin is an excellent way to start."

"He's not waiting for me on the phone now, is he?"

"No. He said you'd been cut off. I told him we've been having some trouble with the phone."

"Thanks," I muttered.

"I don't like to lie, Jeff."

"I know, Dad. I'm sorry. Can I sleep now?"

Dad hesitated. "No. You're going to come downstairs and eat your dinner. And then we can watch a movie, or play cards or do *something*. I'm tired of you using this room as an escape."

"Dad," I said. "Instead of the movie or whatever,

can I get rid of all this stuff?" I waved an arm to indicate the posters, the pictures, the eighth grade schoolbooks, the museum of the person I used to be.

Dad reached over and snapped on my bedside lamp. "That's a great idea," he said. "This is a thirteen-year-old's room, and you're sixteen. That's part of the problem, isn't it?"

That wasn't nearly the whole story, but I nodded.

"Okay." He smiled. "But come down and finish your dinner, all right?"

"Yeah, okay, but one more thing?"

"Yes?"

"The presents." I gestured toward the closet. The presents were still in there, untouched by me.

Dad was quiet for a moment. "I'm sorry," he said finally. "I should have cleared those out. I don't know what I was thinking. They were some kind of charm, I suppose, to bring you back. I should have—"

"Can we give them away? To a hospital or a kids' home or something?"

"Yes," Dad said. "That's a good idea."

I HAD EXPECTED BRIAN TO BE SCARED OF ME AFTER our "Staredown" game, but he had been his usual self the next day, maybe a little more subdued. He continued, in fact, to trail after me like a lost puppy, the same way he related to Dad.

Rejection feels like home to him.

Brian watched me constantly when he thought I wasn't looking. When I caught him at it, he would whip his head around and pretend he'd actually been looking at, say, Jack the cat.

He irritated the hell out of me, but the little conscience I had left told me that except for Connie, Brian irritated the hell out of everyone.

Who cares? Life is hard. He's got to figure it out for himself.

But how could Brian figure anything out when he spent his time sniffing after Dad, who seemed to regard him as something like a mosquito, or me, who wanted nothing to do with him?

As if he sensed my thoughts, Brian came over to the couch I was slouching on. He stood in front of me, one leg crossed in front of the other, wringing his hands nervously.

"What?" I asked sharply, then sat up a little. "Sorry." He smiled, a quick smile that snapped right back off his face. "What do you want, Brian?"

"Well . . . " He took a deep breath. "I was wondering, do you want to play Frisbee with me? I'm pretty good," he boasted, adding quickly, "not like you, though. You're probably a lot better, but . . . "

I sighed. "Frisbee? Where?"

Brian's grin returned, still tentative. "Just out in the yard," he said. "Do you want to?"

No. No, I did not. But I also did not want to spend any more time with him that involved close contact, and at least with Frisbee we would be outside, separated by the throwing distance.

And he could get away from me if he had to.

"Okay, meet me out there," I told Brian.

He clapped his hands once. "All right!"

Dad called to me from his office as I passed. I stopped, keeping one hand on the door frame.

"Going out to play Frisbee?" I nodded. "Would you like me to play too?" I stared at Dad, not sure what he was talking about.

"Frisbee," he said hesitantly. "Outside . . . "

I closed my eyes for a moment when I realized that I had not been outside once without Dad since I had come home.

"No," I said. "You know, Brian . . . " I tilted my head toward the front door and rolled my eyes.

"Yeah, he can be a pest, all right," Dad said, smiling. I felt guilty and looked around for Connie, hoping she hadn't heard. "He's not bothering you too much, is he? I can talk to him."

"Dad . . . " I started, not sure how to put it.

You can't fix everything for me.

"No, it's fine," I said. He nodded quickly.

It was sunny outside, not warm, but not freezing either. Brian stood under the oak tree in the front yard, clutching a bright orange Frisbee. He smiled when he saw me, waving and calling my name.

God, is he really eleven? Was I that young at eleven?

"Hi," I said, forcing a smile to my lips, coming down the steps slowly, a little scared despite myself.

"C'mon, Jeff, let's play!" Brian flipped the Frisbee at me, trying to catch me offguard. I reached up and snagged it, flipping it back to him lightly, happy that my toss was on target.

"Throw it hard, Jeff," Brian yelled, running toward the edge of the yard, flipping the Frisbee wildly back at me. It soared straight up in the air, landing behind Brian in the vacant lot.

"The wind must have got that one," he said, running into the lot to retrieve it.

"Yeah, must have," I agreed, straight-faced.

Brian was hopeless at Frisbee. He kept trying to throw as hard as he could, not understanding that Frisbee required a certain amount of precision. Our game wound up with me standing and watching him as he flipped the Frisbee high in the air, out into the street, against our house, anywhere but at me.

"Brian," I said finally, hesitating when I saw he was almost in tears. "Look, I can show you a few things—"

"You don't need to show me," Brian yelled, backing up, clutching the Frisbee. "I can do it."

"But . . . " I shrugged. If he wanted my help he'd ask for it. I walked over to the porch steps and sat down. Brian watched me for a moment, then trotted over.

"You're not quitting, are you?" he asked, his voice spiraling into a whine.

"I think you need to practice a little more before we play."

Brian looked at the ground. "I'm good," he mumbled.

"No, you're not," I said. He looked up quickly. "That doesn't mean you can't get better. It's just a skill you learn. The first thing is, in Frisbee aim is way more important than power. Until you can get the Frisbee to go where you want, how hard you throw it doesn't mean anything."

He watched me carefully. "That's what Dad said."

I held back a smile, wondering how long Dad could have lasted in a game of Frisbee with Brian. "Well, he's right. You want to try again?" Brian nodded.

I stood next to him in the yard, cocking my wrist to one side. He held the Frisbee awkwardly in the same position, practically straight up and down.

"No, hold your wrist down a little . . . not that much! Okay, not bad. Now flip it *lightly* forward."

Straining, Brian tossed the Frisbee. It wobbled and fell to the ground a few inches in front of us.

"See!" he said, "I can't do it!" He turned away, his face red. I wanted to turn Brian around and show him what he had done, but I was afraid to put my hands on him.

"Brian. Brian!" I called as he hid his face from me. "Hey. That throw was the best one you've done today."

"Oh yeah," he said, turning back with a sneer. "That was the faggiest one I've done today."

I froze, feeling the color drain from my face. I watched him carefully. But Brian wasn't interested in me. He was furious with himself.

Don't be so paranoid. It's just an expression. He doesn't know. No one does.

Everyone does.

"I'm going in now," I said.

Brian focused his attention back on me. "No, don't go in, Jeff, please? I'll listen to you," he begged. "Really."

There was nothing to do inside but sit and think. I could also count on Dad asking why I had come in so soon. I picked up the Frisbee again.

"Okay," I said. "See, when you threw last time, yeah, it didn't go far, but it went straight." I demonstrated, flipping the Frisbee a few inches away. It landed softly on a small pile of dried leaves. "Try it a few more times, and see what happens."

"Okay, Jeff," he said eagerly. I stood back and watched him. After he hit five good throws in a row, I clapped for him. Brian blushed, grinning.

"All right, let's try to play a little. *Gently*," I stressed. "I'll stand a few feet away, and you toss the Frisbee to me."

Brian undershot me, then overshot me, the throw sailing way over my head, but his third try was perfect.

"Hey, that's great, Brian," I said. "Good job!" I flipped it back to him and he tried leaping into the air to catch my gentle toss, tripping over his feet and falling in a heap. This time he laughed, and I laughed with him.

"Hey! Jeff," someone called from behind me. I whirled around and saw a tall, broad-shouldered young guy walking toward us through the vacant lot across the street. Though I would not have recognized him, I knew it had to be Vin.

"Hi, Vin!" Brian scrambled to his feet, intercepting Vin as he reached the lawn. "Hey, I can play Frisbee good now. See?" He jumped around, tossing the Frisbee too hard toward the tree. It went flying down the street and Brian ran after it, calling back over his shoulder, "Don't go anywhere without me!"

Vin walked up to me, his last few steps tentative as I did not return his smile. "Hey, Jeff," he tried again. "How's it going?" I just looked at him.

Vin had always been an inch or so taller than me, and he still was. He also had a good thirty pounds on me now, all muscle, and I noticed a dark shadow of beard on his face. Next to him I felt like a child.

"So," he said, after a long pause, "I can't believe it. My mom said you changed . . . I guess we both have. I missed you, y'know." Vin lurched forward suddenly, putting his arms around me in a brief embrace. Frozen with shame, I could not respond. The idea of responding filled me with horror.

Vin stepped back awkwardly, turning his head away. Looking down the street after Brian, he wiped a hand across his eyes.

He can't be crying. For me? Why?

"Um," I started, intending to tell him that I had to go in now—

To do what?

"It's good to see you, but . . . "

Brian raced up to us, panting. "Hey, Vin," he yelled, so loudly I winced, "want to play Frisbee with us?"

"Well," Vin said, glancing at me. "Uh, I kind of thought me and Jeff could take a walk over to the high school—if he wants. I was going to shoot some baskets myself, and I thought maybe . . . " He stopped, this more than half-grown man I didn't know.

"I can't," I said, meeting Vin's eyes for a second, then looking past him. "I have to stay around here— you know." I gestured back toward the house and saw Dad standing at the living room window, watching us. Watching me. Humiliated, I kicked at the ground until I noticed Vin staring at me.

"Well, okay," he said, "but how about if I come in for a few minutes? You know, just to talk a little."

"Yeah," Brian said, "we can play Monopoly. Or Clue. Which do you like better, Vin?"

"Well . . . " Vin glanced at Brian, then at me, trying a half smile.

The front door opened and Dad called out, "Vin! Good to see you." He came down the walkway and stood next to me, placing his hand on my shoulder. I looked down, wanting to shake him off, but comforted in some way by his presence.

Vin brightened, flashing a smile at Dad. "Hi, Mr. Hart. I just came over to see if Jeff wanted to play basketball with me at the high school. I'm parked over there. I mean, if it's okay with you."

"Jeff said he had to stay home," Brian piped up, "but he doesn't, right, Dad?"

I cursed myself for having anything to do with Brian.

"Well . . . " Dad hesitated. "I'm not sure. Jeff, do you want to go out with Vin?"

I looked at him quickly, wondering if I'd heard correctly: *Do I want to go out with Vin?* His look back was troubled, but innocent.

I didn't know what to say, or what I wanted to do, other than disappear and magically find myself in my bed under the covers. That wasn't going to happen.

"Can I go too?" Brian begged, eyes widening in shock when Dad, Vin and I all said yes.

Brian trotted along ahead of us, looking back every so often to make sure we were following him. I felt excruciatingly self-conscious. Vin had picked up on my nervousness. He was silent too, and he avoided looking at me. But his shoulders were back, his head held high, and he walked with an easy pride and confidence I envied.

"You said you were parked around here," I said as we neared the high school. "Does that mean you have a car?"

Vin looked over at me, smiling. "Yeah. A truck. My uncle helped me buy it. Wait'll you see it."

I didn't respond, more alienated than before. I did not even know how to drive.

"Hey, Brian," Vin yelled. "Show Jeff my truck." Brian looked back at us, then ran ahead to a late-model red Toyota parked in the student lot on the edge of the Wayne High campus. I looked at Vin questioningly.

"I took Brian for a ride once, the first day I got the truck. He saw me driving by your house and he flagged me down. Your dad gave me this lecture afterward—I guess Brian and Charlie aren't supposed to go anywhere without telling him."

Unaccountably moved, I was able to forget myself for a moment. "Thanks for taking time with Brian. Charlie too. I know you talk to her at school sometimes."

Vin frowned, nodding awkwardly. "Oh yeah, that's nothing."

"Okay, but I appreciate it."

"Well, of course," Vin said, still frowning. "I mean, we were friends, and I hope we can be again, and—aaggh! This is too much emotion for me."

I laughed, relieved. "Me too. So . . . this is your truck." Brian had climbed into the bed of the truck and was standing tall, looking in every direction.

"Yeah," Vin said, running his hand lovingly over the hood. "I have to work all the time to support it, but it's worth it. There's nothing like being your own boss, going wherever you want."

I watched him, wanting to touch the truck too, but feeling too shy to do it.

Vin glanced up at me, smiling. "You want to go somewhere later, after we play?"

"Where?" I didn't want to go to his house, where we might meet his mother or one of his brothers. Or worse, where I might have to be alone with him.

"Nowhere far, or anything," Vin said, his smile fading. "We could just get something to eat at Taco Bell or McDonalds or wherever."

"Yeah," Brian said, inviting himself along.

I shrugged, not committing, wanting to say no.

The basketball courts were built into the hill at the back end of the high school campus, next to the football bleachers. We sprinted up the bleachers, giving Brian a twenty-second head start. As he crowed from the top step, Vin came in second, close behind him. I was a distant third, my leg muscles cramping as I joined them on the top step. I stamped my feet in place, trying to catch my breath.

"You've got to be kidding!" Vin said, smiling uneasily. "I could never beat you in a race."

"I would have beat you even without a head start," Brian boasted.

"Yeah, probably." I looked away from both of them.

"Well . . . " Vin said finally, "you want to play?"

"Yeah!" Brian said, racing over to the railings that separated the bleachers from the courts. He clambered over them, looking back for us.

"Okay," I shrugged. Vin nodded, watching me carefully.

Once we started playing basketball, an easy game of Horse, our awkwardness faded a little. The conversation centered around what we were doing, and Brian was happy to take up any slack. Soon Vin and I fell into a comfortable silence, just goofing around shooting free throws, giving Brian the extra shots he demanded without bothering to argue with him.

"So what teams are you on?" I asked Vin after a while, rocketing a set shot that hit the rim, spun and went in.

"Football in winter, baseball in spring. Not basketball. I just do that for fun. Hey," he said abruptly, "when are you coming back to school?"

"I don't know," I said with no enthusiasm.

"You don't know?" Vin looked surprised. "You are coming back, right? I mean, you have to."

"I suppose . . . " I said, trailing off.

"But . . . " Vin hesitated. "I mean, what else can you do?"

"I don't know," I said irritably.

"I'd help you," Vin said. "You know, getting started and all that. I could introduce you around . . . you know most of the guys I hang out with anyway. They're the same friends we had at Wayne Elementary."

I kept my face blank, knowing I would never, ever fit comfortably into a group of guys again.

"Besides, you can't go out for baseball if you're not in school. You are getting back into baseball, right?" Vin's voice was casual, but he stopped and held the ball to wait for my answer.

"Give me the ball, Vin," Brian said, holding out his hands. Vin tossed it to him without looking.

"Let's sit on the bleachers," he said. "I'm tired." He didn't look tired at all, but I was sweating and shivering at the same time. I started to protest, but shrugged, figuring he was right. *I* was tired.

"Brian, you keep playing, okay?" Vin said over his shoulder.

"Yeah, I'm gonna practice my free throw," he called. I heard him hit the rim and curse as the ball missed.

Vin sprawled out across the top step. After a moment I sat down in the same row, leaving plenty of space between us.

"You don't look too good," Vin said bluntly, turning to face me. "You're too skinny. You don't have any endurance. There's nothing wrong with you, is there?"

No, see, it's just that I wasn't supposed to get out of arm's reach of Ray, and he didn't exactly take me jogging, you know?

"I'm okay," I said.

"So, are you going out for baseball in the spring?"

"No," I said definitively. Vin stared at me. "Like you said," I added quickly, "I'm not exactly ready for that."

Vin looked out at the field, one hand over his eyes to protect him from the sun. "It's December. Practice starts in three months. You have plenty of time to get in shape. I'll help you. We could work out together." I winced, but he didn't see. "We've got a good team. I'm on varsity. You could be too, with your arm."

"What's the coach like?" I asked, for lack of anything else to say.

"A hardass. A jerk. He takes everything too seriously and thinks he's God. But he's a good coach. When I made varsity last year, he gave me a rough time, but it wasn't for nothing. I mean, he really tested me out, found out where he thought I'd do the best and put me at third."

I shrugged, listening to him, knowing I would never set foot on a playing field again.

"Don't rule it out, Jeff," Vin said. I looked at him, raising my eyebrows. "Baseball. I mean, what's the point of not—"

"I've had enough of hardass jerks," I told him, biting off the words, realizing too late I had opened the door to other questions I did not want to answer.

Vin looked at me cautiously. "You're talking about that guy, aren't you? The one who kidnapped you."

"Yeah," I said. "That's who I'm talking about."

"So they got him," Vin said, but his tone was questioning. "I saw it on the news. He was following you or something, in San Francisco."

"Yeah," I said abruptly.

"He's in jail, right?" I nodded. "He's going to stay there? I mean—"

"Look, Vin, I don't know much more about that than you do. And I don't want to talk about it."

"Sure, sure," he said, backing off. I waited. "Only—"

"What?" I said, my voice as cold as I could make it.

"Listen," he said, "you don't have to answer this. But a lot of people are wondering, did that guy molest you?"

Here it was. The question left me unmoved. I knew what Vin wanted to hear. What he had to hear.

"He never touched me."

"He didn't?" Vin hesitated, squinting at me. "Okay, that's good enough for me."

Oh, it's good enough for you, is it?

I felt the distance between us.

If you knew, Vin . . .

"I want you to come back to school. I have people I

hang out with now, but that's all they are. They're not friends like you and I were friends."

I shrugged. "It depends on what my dad wants, I guess."

He looked at me, disappointed. "You'll let me know, right? Call me or something?"

"Yeah," I said listlessly, retreating from him.

A few days before vacation ended, Dad decided to take me to Modesto so I could cash in the gift certificates he and Connie had given me for Christmas.

Thirty-five miles of agricultural land separated Wayne from the nearest town. I focused on the scenery, trying to ignore the glances Dad kept shooting at me. Finally, as we entered Oakdale, he let me know what was on his mind.

"What would you think about my going back to work?" When I didn't answer right away, Dad laughed self-consciously. "I bet you'd be relieved. I know I hover over you too much."

I protested halfheartedly. He shook his finger at me, smiling. "I do, and I know I do. You're very special to me, you know." I was embarrassed, and I guess Dad was too, for he concentrated on the road and didn't say anything else.

"Thanks," I said belatedly when I realized how my silence might be taken. But I mumbled the word, looking away from him.

Dad's next glance at me was anxious. "I am going back to work, Jeff. Monday after New Year's."

"Okay," I said quickly.

"And you're going back to school—"

"Not right then?" I said, panicked.

"No." Dad cleared his throat. "I called the Wayne High principal yesterday. Stan Dodson. He turned out to be a pretty reasonable guy."

I gave a little grunt to keep him talking, but I was shrinking inside.

"He said you could go ahead and start second semester, about three weeks from now. The alternative would be starting you on independent study right away. That's what he recommended at first. But I don't want that for you, Jeff. You need to be back in school."

"I don't want to be a freshman, Dad," I said, grasping at any straw. "I'm too old for that."

"You're going in as a junior. I made sure of that. After all," he said, voice tightening, "it wasn't your fault you missed out on the first two years of high school. Dodson said they could consider you a kind of exchange student. If you keep up with your class, and I know you will, he'll waive the requirements you've missed."

I laughed sharply. "Is that what the kids are going to think? That I'm an 'exchange student'?" Despite my words, I felt hope stirring. The idea of going back to school was terrifying, but Vin was right, what else could I do?

"The other kids will take their cues from you," Dad

said. "If you walk onto that campus knowing you be-long there, you'll be accepted just as you should be."

I shook my head. "It's not going to be that easy."

"Going back to school will be a challenge for you. No question. But I know you, and I know you'll suc-ceed."

You don't know me at all.

"You're going to do fine this year, and next, and you'll graduate with your class. After that, college—"

"College!"

"It's not so far away. Just a year and a half. I can see you going to Berkeley. That's where I went, you know, for college and law school. We'll move back to the Bay Area then, so you can live at home and commute."

"Dad . . . "

What about the rest of the family? Connie has a job here. Charlie does too, and she already thinks you don't give a damn about anyone but me. Brian's messed up enough as it is without uprooting him to make my life more comfortable. And me. College? Dad, you're kidding yourself. I'm an eighth-grade dropout. How . . . ?

"Connie's going to pick up some skills packets for you from the high school next week. I'm sure your read-ing comprehension is fine, but you'll need to get up to speed on math."

"Dad, I don't—"

"Connie and I will help you study. Charlotte's a straight-A student. She can help too. You're a smart kid, Jeff," he said firmly. "I know you can pick up the traces." End of discussion.

Dad smiled over at me as we hit Modesto, the "big city" where Wayne residents shopped for better quality clothes and big-ticket items like cars and computers. Our destination was Vintage Faire, a huge covered mall built on the site of a former almond orchard.

"I'm glad you had a chance to spend some time with Vin the other day. When are you going to see him again?"

"I don't know. I guess I'm supposed to call him or something."

"Vin is a good kid," Dad said. "Do you know he called or came over nearly every week for close to a year after you disappeared? I never had anything new to tell him."

"Vin's a good guy," I said, squirming. "But he's got other friends now. Other jocks. That's what I mean about school. I don't want to tag along after Vin, or have him feel like he has to carry me."

"You know," Dad said abruptly, "one of the things I hate about that man"—I knew he meant Ray—"is the way he robbed you of your confidence. Why don't you have faith in yourself, Jeff? You know you don't need to worry about Vin's friendship, or about making new friends. You'll start school, you'll do well, you'll work your way back into sports, and—"

"How disappointed would you be if I never played sports again?"

We had reached Vintage Faire. Dad pulled into a spot in the underground garage near Macy's. He took his time answering my question.

"I'd be very disappointed, but not for the reasons you think. I'd be disappointed because you'd be giving up on yourself for no good reason. You enjoyed sports, especially baseball. I know I pushed you, but only because you were *good*, and because you loved it. Didn't you?"

I nodded. "Yeah, but things are different now. I'm a different person."

Dad sighed. He clasped the steering wheel for a moment, then looked over at me. "I hate to see you do this to yourself. What does that mean, you're a 'different person?' So different that you can't return to the things you loved? If you're worried about fitting in socially, there's no better way than succeeding in sports. And you *will* succeed, you know that. It's just a matter of getting back into shape. Vin can help you with that, I'm sure, and I'll work with you on weekends."

I felt trapped and overwhelmed. "Dad, I can't play sports anymore."

"Why, for God's sake?"

Suddenly I was so tired of lying. "Because I can't get undressed in front of other people."

A pause. The other noises in the parking garage disappeared as I focused in on the sound of Dad's breathing.

"That's ridiculous. Why not?" Dad's voice still held a trace of bluster, but I heard the fear there too.

"I have marks on my back," I whispered, covering my face with my hands. My stomach felt hollow.

"Marks? What are you talking about?"

"Ray hit me. He left marks. Scars."

"Let me see."

I turned to him in horror. "Dad, no! Please."

"Jeff, let me see." He reached out for me, grabbing at my shoulder.

"No!" I said, pulling away so violently I banged my other shoulder against the door. I swore softly at the pain, steeling myself for Dad to come at me again.

"I'm sorry," he said after a long moment. I gave a shrug that felt more like a convulsive twitch. Dad reached up to wipe his forehead, and I saw that his hand was shaking.

"Why . . . what would he use to leave scars? Jesus," he whispered.

Powerful images washed over me, and I was no longer in the car with Dad.

"A whip," I said. "He used a whip." My voice sounded calm enough, but saying the words out loud shocked me. I began to cry as I never wanted to do around my father. He leaned over, pulling me close, wrapping his arms around my trembling body.

I tolerated the embrace at first, too weak to deny him a third time. But then I couldn't breathe. "Let me go, Dad," I said, my voice muffled against his chest. He loosened his grip, but didn't release me.

"What, Jeff, I didn't hear—"

"Goddamn you," I cried, wrenching myself out of

his arms, "let go of me!" Dad sat back in shock, staring at me.

"Sorry," I tossed at him after a moment. "I shouldn't have—"

"Forget about that," Dad said in a tone that shut me up immediately. "We're not through talking about Slaight."

Yes, we are.

Dad took a deep breath. "You're saying Slaight beat you." I nodded. "You're telling me he used a *whip* on you?" I nodded again, disgusted with myself, prickles of heat breaking out across my body. "But . . ." Dad sputtered. "Why? *Why* would he do that?"

"I don't know, okay?" Fresh tears came to my eyes. I blinked them back angrily, wiping a hand across my face. Dad pushed a handkerchief on me and I took it without looking at him. "I don't know why he did it. He was mad at me, I guess."

Ray lay next to me on the bed, crying, holding a cold towel to my forehead as I shivered and burned with fever.

"I'm sorry, baby," he said. "Don't die on me."

"He didn't mean to hurt me that bad," I said, staring down at my hands. "He was sorry for it later."

Dad cleared his throat. "Does Dave know about this?"

"No. Not from me," I added, then flushed.

Yeah, like Ray told him.

"Well, he'll have to know," Dad said grimly. "I'll

tell him when he calls tonight. He'll want to talk to you too."

"No. I don't want to talk about it anymore. I wish I hadn't told you."

But the marks were there. I could feel them. Ugly. Hideous.

"Okay," Dad said quietly, sounding like he was talking to himself. "This is tough. This is . . . " He clenched his hands into fists, and I flinched. "I think you need to talk about this stuff, Jeff. To me, to Dave, to . . . somebody."

"No," I said. "There's nothing more to tell."

"You have to live your life," Dad said suddenly, "and Ray Slaight is not a part of it anymore. You're not going to let him stop you from going to school or playing sports—or doing anything else you want to do."

There's nothing I want to do.

"We've got to get you to a doctor," Dad muttered. "I've put it off too long."

"I don't need a doctor," I said, gathering control of myself. "It . . . my back . . . it happened a long time ago. Ray took care of it. I'm fine."

" 'Ray took care of it,' " Dad repeated in a low voice. "Great. Terrific." He took a deep breath. "Tell me this. Did he hurt you in other ways?"

"Dad!" I burst out, suddenly not afraid of him, not even a little bit. "Leave me alone about this."

He nodded immediately. "All right, Jeff. All right."

We sat in tense silence for some minutes, each of us

staring straight ahead. Finally I sighed, and that seemed to break Dad's reserve.

"So," he said with forced cheer, "how about getting some lunch inside the mall? Connie says there's a good Italian place here. We can shop afterward."

"Okay," I said. "Sure."

We got out of the Jeep and walked toward the mall entrance. Not communicating.

DAD LOOKED IN ON ME AT DAWN THE MORNING he was to return to work. He walked quietly to my bed, a small, yellow legal pad in his hand. Tense, not sure what he had in mind, I briefly considered faking sleep. But I didn't, watching him until he met my eyes.

"Jeff. I didn't know you were up. I hope I didn't wake you." Dad sounded formal, distant, the way he had ever since we had talked about my back. Or not talked about my back.

"I was already awake," I said, hating the eagerness in my voice. Eager to please. Eager to apologize.

"Well, then," Dad said, hitting the legal pad once sharply against his other hand. "I have a list of numbers here where you can reach me today. If you need anything, or just . . . " He trailed off, looking at a point somewhere over my shoulder.

"I'll be okay, Dad." He didn't answer. "I'll be fine."

"All right." He set the pad on my bedside table. "Anyway, you have these now. I'll see you tonight."

I lay awake after that, listening to the sounds of the others waking up. Connie and Brian left the house next, together, headed for Wayne Elementary School. Forty-five minutes after that Charlotte took off, and I was alone in the house for the first time since I had returned.

I considered spending the day in bed, but it was no use. I had grown too accustomed to the early morning routine Dad had set with me. At nine I went downstairs to find breakfast. Jack the cat, who had long since grown used to my presence, trailed after me hopefully. I knelt and rubbed his chin, which he stretched up to me, the better for my fingers to reach.

After a bowl of Cheerios, I wondered what to do with the rest of the day. I thought about walking into town just to get some exercise, but I didn't want to risk any "Welcome back!" conversations with anyone who used to know me. I also didn't want to run into an authority figure of any kind wondering why I wasn't in school.

Finally I settled onto the couch for some daytime TV—game shows or soap operas, anything mindless. Within five minutes though, my eyelids were heavy and I felt sleep coming with an ease I never experienced at night. Leaving the TV on for white noise, I stretched out full-length on the sofa, moving my body to fit around the cat curled up beside me.

Someone was shaking my foot. I groaned, turning on my side, wanting back into the best sleep I'd had since I'd come home.

"Hey, Jeff," Vin said, laughing a little.

Instantly awake, I sat up, drawing my foot back

from his hand. He stood at the other end of the couch, looking embarrassed, Charlie and a short, dark-haired girl flanking him.

"I wish I could sleep in like that," Vin said, trying a laugh again. Charlie and the girl agreed, laughing with him.

"It's lunchtime," Charlie said, smiling nervously. "Sherry and I usually eat lunch here. Vin came over with us today. . . . " She trailed off at my lack of response.

"Hi," Sherry said, stepping forward. I stood to meet her. "You're Jeff, I'm Sherry. How's it going?" Sherry was petite, shorter than Charlie by at least two inches, slim and pretty with big dark eyes.

"Okay," I said, relaxing at the casual way she'd greeted me. "How's it going with you?" She shrugged and smiled, apparently not caring that I was a celebrity/freak.

"Whatever. Charlie, do you still have Mountain Dew? I need a rush."

"She's cute, huh?" Vin said after the girls had left.

"Sherry? Yeah, I guess." I met his eyes and he smiled.

"Yeah, Charlie's pretty cute, too."

"Why don't you ask her out," I said, surprising myself. "She'd love it."

"Charlie? Nah. I mean, she's pretty and everything, but that would be like dating my sister." We stood quietly for a moment, not looking at each other.

"Anyway," Vin said finally, clearing his throat,

"You want to go get lunch at Burger King or McDonald's? My truck's outside."

The traffic up to East Wayne was hell, but Vin decided to drive out to McDonald's anyway. After we got our food, Vin looked at his watch and laughed.

"There's no way I'm going to get back in time for calculus."

"You're not? What else do you have after lunch?"

He made a face. "English. It sucks. We have to write about our *feelings* all the time."

"How are you doing in school?" In elementary school, it had always been a struggle for Vin to maintain a C average so he could play sports. We had done our homework together almost every night at one or the other's house.

"I do okay. It's not easy. I don't mind math or science, but English . . . "

I smiled at him. "Sounds like before."

"Yeah, my grades were shot to hell for a while after you left." He frowned and took a ferocious bite out of his Quarter Pounder.

"So, did someone else—"

"What, work with me?" He laughed to himself. "I had a girlfriend freshman year who said she'd do my homework for me. I let her. It turned out she was dumber than me. I knew I could get better than D's on my own, so I started to put in the time. It's a habit now." After sipping his Coke down to the dregs, he tossed the empty cup onto the tray. "You done? Let's drive up to the snow."

The snow line began about fifteen miles east of Wayne, as the foothills faded into the Sierra Nevada Mountains. Once Vin reached the Twain Harte Grade where the road split, he checked his rearview mirror for the Highway Patrol, then sped up, revving the truck up the grade. I laughed, exhilarated. At the top of the grade, where the road narrowed and the pine trees closed in on either side, Vin slowed, but not by much.

"That day you disappeared," he said abruptly. "That was a crazy day. You were supposed to pitch that night, remember?"

I tried to keep the irony out of my voice. "Yeah. I remember."

Vin glanced over at me, then back at the road. "You didn't show up at the game, no one knew why. I went to your house, no one was there. Next morning, still no one. Finally it was all over the news about you. Your dad was on TV, on all the stations, asking whoever took you just to let you go." He slowed a little more, and I watched him. "He stayed in Fresno for a while, trying to find you." Vin glanced at me again. "You ever talk about this with him?"

"No. I don't want to talk about it at all, so—"

"At first the police thought you might be around that rest area somewhere," he continued, ignoring me. "All kinds of people were looking for you there. I felt like if *I* was there I'd find you. You'd be in a ditch or something, hit by a car, nothing too serious, maybe a broken leg . . . it would bug me especially at night. I begged my mom to drive me down there but she wouldn't do it. In the daytime, I could tell myself there were hundreds of people looking in ditches, they'd find you if you were there, but the nights . . . "

I hesitated, moved, not sure what to say. "I know what you mean about nights."

"For a long time I couldn't think about anything else. School was a waste. I picked fights. I cried in class a few times." He worked his shoulders, irritated with himself. "So . . . anyway, that was three years ago, almost. History, right?"

"Right," I agreed. I had wondered what my family and friends were doing while I was with Ray, if they still thought of me as time and distance grew between us. I wanted Vin to catch me up on school, sports and people we both knew. But just as quickly, the urge passed. My questions would only make the contrast between us that much clearer.

We stopped at Little Sweden, a tobogganing hill about twenty miles east of Wayne. Neither Vin nor I were dressed for the weather, but he rented sleds for both of us and we spent the rest of the afternoon sliding down Little Sweden over and over, laughing and acting like kids. We even had a snowball fight, using our sleds as shields, barely able to clasp the snow in our reddened, freezing hands.

The shadows of the pine trees were lengthening on the snow before either of us thought to check the time. It was after four.

On the way back down the hill I told him, "I'll pay you back for this."

"What"—he laughed—"you mean when I got you on the back of the neck—"

"No. For what you spent on the sleds, on lunch today, the other day too."

Vin waved me off as if protesting out loud would be too much trouble.

"No, I want to. I can't have you paying for everything. . . . " I broke off, my face growing hot. Who was I to assume that Vin's sponsorship was going to continue?

"Hey, Jeff." Vin's smile was uneasy now. "What's going on?"

I shook my head. "Nothing. Just tired, I guess." Vin nodded. "It was a great day," I added.

Vin nodded again, solemnly, but did not respond. We rode the rest of the way to the house in silence.

"Well," I said, reaching for the door handle the moment Vin stopped the truck. "I better go in now. See you, okay?"

"Wait a minute," Vin said, laughing self-consciously. "So . . . when am I going to see you again?"

I was quiet, not knowing what to say.

"I can come over for lunch pretty much every day, if you want. Until you come back to school, I mean. Or we could do something on the weekend."

Vin sounded so awkward I was able to put aside my own insecurity for the moment. "Sure, that'd be okay, I guess. Either one."

"Your dad wouldn't mind?"

I looked at him strangely. But he didn't know

about Dad's matchmaking efforts. "No. No, he won't mind."

Dad arrived back from San Francisco after I was already in bed. I could hear him talking to Connie downstairs, not the words, just his tone, which was tired. I sat up, half afraid he would stop in to see me and half fearing that he wouldn't.

Ten minutes later, he appeared in the doorway. "How'd you do today?"

"Okay. Vin came over for lunch," I offered, not bothering to add that he had cut school to take me up to the snow.

Dad put a hand to the back of his neck and stretched. "Good. That's good. He knows you're going back to school?"

"Yeah. He wants to come over and have lunch here every day until then."

Dad shifted as if he couldn't wait to get away. "Great. Glad to hear it. Well . . . " he said, turning to leave.

"Dad!" He turned back to me, an anxious look on his face. I leaned over to snap on the light, then sat up in bed.

"It's nothing," I said, "just, I hate to ask, but can I borrow some money? I owe Vin for lunch and things."

"I'm sorry," Dad said, coming into the room, fumbling for his wallet. "I should have thought." He pulled out two twenties. "Is this enough?"

"Thanks," I said, reaching up to take the money.

"That's really too much. I'll pay you back. I'll . . . I'll get a job or something."

Dad reached down and clapped me on the shoulder, pulling his hand back fast. "Don't rush yourself, Jeff. I'll give you an allowance."

"Whatever you give Charlie is fine," I said shortly. I knew he didn't want to touch me and I felt unclean.

Dad looked confused. "I don't give her money. Connie handles all that."

I didn't answer and he began to look as uncomfortable as I felt. "Well . . . " he said, glancing back toward the hallway.

"I want to earn money for a car," I said abruptly, then looked down. From forty dollars a car will grow. Dumb.

"A car?" Dad thought for a moment. "Well, of course. You're sixteen. Hell, you'll be seventeen in July. You don't know how to drive. . . . " Dad's tone was questioning and I shook my head quickly. "All right. This weekend, I'll give you some driving lessons. We can use the junior college parking lot, maybe play some basketball afterward. Vin can come along, if you want."

He smiled at me, reassured in some way, and I smiled back at him.

DAD TOOK TO THE IDEA OF MY DRIVING LESSONS
with an enthusiasm I could not match. By the end of the
week, I was tense with him, and shy, feeling bound to dis-
appoint. It did not help that Brian invited himself along
for my first lesson, or that Dad insisted I invite Vin.

"Jeff, I have a surprise for you," Dad said as the four
of us left Wayne early Saturday morning.

"What?" I said, trying to smile, apprehensive at the
excitement I heard in his voice.

"Well," Dad was grinning at me. "How would you
like a new car?"

I was silent, trying to absorb his words. Vin reacted
for me, leaning forward, pounding the seat.

"A new car! Wow. What kind, Mr. Hart?"

Dad glanced at me again, then back at Vin. "I know
someone who knows someone with a great deal on a
white Mustang convertible, only a year old."

Vin leaned back. In the mirrored visor I could see
him smiling, shaking his head. "That's great, Mr. Hart.
A white Mustang."

"Jeff?" Dad said, looking at me again, holding on to his grin. "What do you think?"

"You bought me a car?" I said slowly.

"No, no," Dad said, a little edgy now. "I haven't bought anything. It's an idea. Connie thought I should run it by you first."

"I don't want a car," I said tightly, folding my arms across my chest. Everyone was silent. "I mean"— I ventured a glance at him—"thanks, and everything, but . . . "

Dad's face was grim as he watched the road.

"I don't even know how to drive," I said, trying to laugh, to win him back.

"You're going to learn," Dad said, eager again. "It won't take long, and then you'll have this great car for school."

"We live less than a mile from Wayne High, though," I couldn't stop myself from pointing out.

"You'll use it for college then. Come on, kid, get excited."

"I am, Dad. I am. Only . . . maybe we could wait on the car? Just for a while?"

"Tell you what, Jeff, I'll tell the guy we're interested. He's not in a big hurry to sell it, and if I put a deposit down . . . "

"Okay, Dad." I smiled at him. "Great. Whenever. No hurry."

He frowned, and I cursed myself for saying the wrong thing again.

Vin was watching me from the backseat. I knew what he was thinking.

Your dad wants to give you a new car, and you don't even want it? What's wrong with you?

"Okay, guys, here's the plan," Dad said, clearing his throat. "We'll hit Redbird College first, let Jeff get some driving in, then play some basketball out there. After that we'll pick a spot for lunch. How does that sound?"

After an awkward silence, Vin said, "Sounds great, Mr. Hart."

Redbird College was just three miles outside Wayne. Whoever had designed the college had preserved the beauty and rural atmosphere of the area: the classroom buildings were constructed from redwood, and they blended into the surrounding woods almost as if they belonged there. The layout of the campus followed the hilly site where it had been built, and consequently any trip to the college involved some major climbing.

There were actually three parking lots, built on graduated levels. Dad parked at the very end of the highest lot, lifting his hands from the wheel with a flourish.

"It's all yours," he said. There was an awkward moment when he didn't move and I wondered if I was supposed to slide under him. But then Dad remembered, opening the door quickly and stepping out of the Jeep.

"Wait for me," he ordered, and shut the door to walk around. Sighing, I slid over.

"Jeff, something going on?" Vin asked in a low voice.

I shook my head, forcing a smile back at him over my shoulder. "Nah."

Dad opened the passenger-side door and climbed in. "All right, Jeff. Start 'er up!"

"Okay." I knew he was angry about the car. I could hear it in his voice, beneath the forced cheer. Grimacing, I turned the Jeep's key too far, grinding the gears. Dad winced, visibly collecting himself. "Sorry," I said quickly, but he waved off the apology, nodding for me to try again.

Driving was a disaster. Though the Jeep was an automatic, I couldn't seem to remember which gear to leave it in, or how to stop the vehicle without throwing everyone forward, or how to maneuver around parked cars without giving Dad fits. In the backseat, Vin and Brian took on the status of Olympic judges, and their silence at my incompetence was more telling than insults would have been.

To compensate for the near misses I'd been having, I slowed way down, driving about ten miles an hour. Finally, I felt some control over what I was doing. Concentrating on what was right in front of me, I drove slow and straight through the top parking lot, making an exaggeratedly wide turn to accommodate the short jog down to the second lot.

The second level parking lot was much narrower than the first, and I slowed down even more. I heard a small sigh of boredom escape Brian's lips, but I ignored it, putting through the lot about five miles an hour.

"Jeff," Dad said finally, breaking the silence. "You know, you can go a little faster. It's okay—it's safe."

The word hit me like a fist. "Safe?" I looked over at him, and the car followed my eyes.

"Jeff's gonna hit that guy!" Brian yelled, and I jumped on the brakes, looking up to see a thin, bearded man on a bicycle glaring back at me over his shoulder as he pedaled off.

All was quiet in the Jeep. Then Dad sighed. "Look, I know you have good intentions, but just . . . speed it up a little, all right?"

"I almost killed that guy!" I shot back, my heart still in my throat. My voice broke a little and I looked down.

God, I'm an idiot.

"You weren't anywhere near him," Vin said mildly. I glanced up to the mirror again. "You were at least six feet away. He probably just heard Brian yelling." I tightened my fingers around the steering wheel, then relaxed them, nodding once at Vin.

Thanks.

"So," Dad said heartily, "let's try it again, hey?"

I shook my head. "I don't want to do this anymore."

"Now, Jeff," Dad said, cajoling, "once more around. Let's just get back to where we started." Disgusted with his tone of voice, I started to answer him back.

Hey, I'm not five, okay?

But I answered myself back—

Then don't act like you are. Not in front of Vin.

I sat up, taking a deep breath, and took my foot off the brake. I made it through the second lot without further event, then down to the third and final level. Holding the steering wheel in a death grip, I motored back up to the highest lot, maintaining a speed of about five miles an hour the whole time. We had no more near misses, but Dad never stopped watching me. I pulled into our original parking spot, shut the motor off smoothly and handed the keys to him. Dad hesitated before he spoke.

"Well," he said finally. "Yes. That's enough for now. That was a good effort. Next time we'll—"

"I don't want to do this anymore," I said loudly. "I don't want to drive, I don't want a car, I don't want . . . this." I stepped out of the Jeep without waiting for his response. Looking around, I wanted to run away from him, from all of them. But where was I supposed to go? I remembered—

—driving with Ray. Out in the desert, just after dawn. It is cold, my arms and legs covered with gooseflesh even as I savor the rare comfort of the car's plush upholstery against them. Ray takes the deserted highway at eighty, eighty-five, ninety . . . and I stop looking.

He reaches out, grabbing my upper thigh high under my shorts. I tense, drawing in my breath, and Ray lifts his other hand from the wheel. He steers with his knees, laughing as we weave across both lanes of the highway and back again. We are going to crash,

and, amazed, I realize I still care. I smile at Ray, re-
laxing into his touch—

For one terrifying moment nothing changes. Then
he smiles at me and slowly, deliberately, places both
hands back on the steering wheel.

"Jeff!" Dad stood in front of me, staring into my
eyes. I shied away from him, bumping into the Jeep.

"Hey, come back!" he said, laughing awkwardly. I
looked around slowly. Brian stood close by, watching
me, while Vin hung back a little, trying to allow me
some privacy, I felt.

"Yeah, what is it?" I barked at Dad sharply, then retreated. "Sorry. I was daydreaming, I guess."

He nodded, stepping back to give me room. Without
meaning to, I sighed heavily, shaking out my arms and
hands. I felt tight all over, a band of tension across my
shoulders.

"I was just saying"—Dad peered at me again—"that
we might as well leave the Jeep here and walk down to
the courts. It's a ways down, but the walk will do us
good."

The walk will do you good.

I glared at him, not understanding why I was so furious but feeling it nonetheless. "Yeah, the walk'll do us
good," I repeated, horrified when I realized I was imi-
tating him.

Dad tilted his head toward me, frowning, and I prepared myself for a real confrontation with him. With a
sick feeling I understood that was what I wanted. But
then I watched as the fight drained out of him, his

shoulders slumping. He turned away and began walking toward the stairs that led down to the second parking level. Brian trotted after him, glancing back at me.
Vin looked at me, wordless.

"I don't want to fucking be here," I said to myself,
startled when Vin nodded.

"Yeah . . . " Vin shuffled a little, not knowing what
to say. He looked after Dad, who was disappearing
down the stairs without a backward glance.

Pretend you're human. Go.

"Come on," I said roughly, then cleared my throat.
Vin turned back, raising his eyebrows. "We better follow them."

"Yeah." Vin looked relieved. We walked together
through the parking lot. Grateful for his silence, I noticed I was matching him stride for stride, keeping up
much more easily than I had the day we'd played basketball together almost three weeks ago. I was safe and
I was home and I was getting stronger. So why did I
still feel mired in shit?

I wasn't much more successful at basketball than I had
been at driving. One bump from Dad was enough; I
didn't want to play anymore. I stood back, hovering
around the edges of the court, pacing, waving off Vin's
and Brian's attempts to throw me the ball. Finally, I
took myself out of the game, and Dad didn't question
me. I sat back against the redwood and hurricane fence
that surrounded the court, knees up, head down. Vin
came over and sat next to me after a while, watching

Brian and Dad as they played game after game of Horse and Poison. I ignored him, simmering, wanting to be left alone but furious that Dad wasn't pushing to see what was wrong with me.

You know what's wrong with you. So does he. The only way to get through it is to pretend that nothing ever happened. But it did. It did.

Dad finally called it a day, heaving with sweat, avoiding my eyes as he declared game, set, match to Brian. Delighted with the extra attention, Brian scampered off after Dad, chattering to him about their games.

I trudged along, Vin keeping pace with me. He still hadn't said anything and I realized how much I appreciated his silent companionship.

"Listen, this day . . . " I looked at him finally, grimacing as we climbed the endless stairs that led to the upper parking lot. "I'm sorry we dragged you along. I mean . . . " I gestured my disgust at myself, at Dad, at everything.

Vin shook his head. "Hey. You should see me when I'm fighting with my mom. It's okay." He stopped on the second-level landing, leaning back against the guard-rail, stretching his arms out. "Let's rest for a minute." Suspicious he had only stopped on my behalf, I was grateful anyway, my lungs aching from the unaccustomed climbing.

"I'm not *fighting* with him," I said, then stopped myself. What was I doing then, if I was not fighting with Dad? Vin was watching me, so I shrugged. "I don't know. It's just a shitty day, I guess." He nodded, and I started climbing again. Vin followed a little reluctantly, and I figured he had more he wanted to say. But what could he say that would mean anything to me?

Dad was standing by the Jeep talking into his cell phone when we made it to the third-level landing. The sight caused me to stop walking, and Vin stumbled into me.

"Sorry," I mumbled, stepping aside fast. Dad caught sight of us and waved urgently, flipping his phone shut. I walked toward him slowly, knowing something bad must have happened, knowing it must involve me, powerless to do anything about it.

"That was Connie. We have to get back," Dad said as we reached the Jeep.

Dread gnawed at my stomach. "Why? What's going on?"

"I'll take you home first, Vin," Dad said, ignoring me.

"Um . . . " Vin hesitated. "My truck—it's parked at your house."

"That's right," Dad said. "Damn it. Well, that can't be helped."

The cell phone rang again as we began the trip back to Wayne. Dad didn't answer it.

The phone rang several more times until Dad finally told Brian to turn off the ringer. Then, a few minutes later, as we were entering the town of Wayne, the car phone rang. Dad sighed, reaching for it.

"Yeah? Yeah, I know. Thanks." He listened, growing more agitated. "Okay. All right. Talk to you later, then." Dad set the phone back with exaggerated care.

Brian broke the silence. "Dad," he said timidly. "Who was on the phone? Was it Mom again?"

Dad waited so long I didn't think he was going to answer. "That was Dave," he said finally. "He's coming up tomorrow to talk to Jeff."

Vin turned to me, mouthing, "Dave?" I ignored him, suddenly cold. Wrapping my arms around my body, I turned away, staring out the window.

"The reporters are back," Dad said flatly. He said it in front of Vin. I hoped I only imagined the disgust I heard in his voice.

THE NEXT MORNING, DAD AND I SPENT A SILENT breakfast together. For some incomprehensible reason he had prepared an elaborate meal: scrambled eggs, bacon, pancakes and rolls. I picked at it only enough to avoid comment, then settled in the living room to wait for Stephens. I wanted to go up to my room but I didn't want to give Dad the chance to attack me again for "escaping."

I had recognized several of the reporters from before; only this time they had harder looks, more of a pushing frenzy when we all emerged from the Jeep. Two of the TV crews had blocked our driveway and Dad had been forced to park on the street.

Silent this time, he had taken my elbow and steered me through the crowd. Cringing without knowing why, I had looked at Dad in mute apology as the reporters called my name, and his. His face wooden, Dad had merely propelled me the rest of the way to the door, looking back only once to bark, "Brian!" Brian had scrambled up the stairs after us, but not before one man's voice stood out of the crowd.

"Jeff, is it true Ray Slaight took nude photos of you?"

Unable to stop myself, I turned around to face my inquisitor as Dad fumbled with the door. As I had thought, it was the pudgy young man who had questioned me before. Standing ahead of the crowd and somehow apart from them, the reporter looked up at me, earnest and relentless.

"Is it true?" he prompted. "Did Slaight take pictures of you?"

Detached as the shock hit me, I shook my head. "No. It's not true."

Dad got the door open and tugged on the back of my jersey, murmuring my name. I sleepwalked the few steps back, Brian pushing past me. As the door shut on the mob, I had caught a glimpse of Vin at its edges, his gaze on me, sharp and speculative.

Ray and I stood in his front room, kissing. He held me close, moving his hands slowly over my body. Pleasure and shame washed over me in almost equal amounts.

Someone was outside, walking toward the house. Unless Ray hurried, he would not finish before the stranger arrived. But I could not rush him and I could not pull away from him. All I could do was live in Ray's time and move to his rhythm.

"Jeff!" Dad shouted, shaking my shoulder. My eyes flew open before I was truly awake. I stared at him, not sure where I was for a moment.

"You were having a nightmare," he said, pushing his hair back. "You must have fallen asleep on the couch."

I sat up, breathing hard, wondering what he had seen.

"Are you all right?" Dad asked roughly. I nodded. "Must have been a bad one. You were . . . you almost fell off the couch, you were moving around so much."

"I'm sorry," I said.

"No, no," Dad said, waving a hand in my direction. He hesitated, looking away. "Listen, Dave is here."

"What?" I said, as my stomach clenched in on itself. "Here? Where?"

"He just pulled up outside," Dad modified. "So . . . get yourself together. You're going to talk to him now."

I didn't like the implied threat in his voice. "I have nothing to say to Stephens."

Or you.

"You are going to talk to him," Dad said. "But . . . go on and pull yourself together."

It was the second time he had said something like that, and I wondered how long he had watched me in my dream that was too close to the reality I had known. Then I realized I was drenched in sweat, far out of proportion to the temperature in the room.

"I'm going upstairs to take a shower," I said, testing him.

Dad nodded without looking at me. "That's fine, Jeff. Go ahead."

As the hot water pounded me, I ran my hands over the ridges in my back, letting myself really feel them for the first time. They felt huge, rough, corded, stretching as far up my spine as I could reach. I grabbed a washcloth off the towel rack, wrapped it around a bar of soap, and scoured my back, rubbing deep and hard.

I stood outside the living room for a moment, leaning my head against the wall, eyes closed. Dad and Stephens spoke so quietly I could not make out what they were saying. But then, afraid I might hear something I could not bear, I stepped into the archway where they could see me.

They stopped talking abruptly. "Come in," Dad said, nodding to me.

Stephens stood next to the picture window, more rumpled than ever. But his eyes were alert, intent on mine.

"Sit down," he said. "We have some things we need to talk about."

When I didn't move, Dad nodded me toward a chair. I hesitated, then sat. Dad and Stephens settled opposite each other on the flanking couches, and I was surrounded.

"What? What is the big dramatic news?" I said too loudly.

"Two days ago we found Slaight's car in San Francisco. The Lexus you described. It was towed out of a private driveway six blocks from your dad's office the same day you saw Slaight. It's been in impound all this time."

I nodded impatiently. "Yeah? You found his car, and . . . ?"

"The officers who searched the car found some photos of you taped under the front seat. Nude photos."

I stared at Stephens, playing his words back in my head. Then, as their impact hit me, I closed my eyes, finally, crushingly, humiliated.

Oh God, Ray, we were driving for hours and you were telling me you loved me and shit and we were sitting—sitting—on those goddamn pictures. You must have been laughing the whole time.

Stephens was calling my name.

"What?" I whispered, my eyes fixed now on the coffee table where Roysten had dumped out my clothes.

"Tell me about the pictures."

I shook my head, clasping my hands tightly together. Out of the corner of my eye I saw Dad shift position.

"*He's* talking, kid." Stephens's voice was gentle. "Did you know that? He's got a whole story about those pictures and how they came to be."

I sank back into the chair, as weakened as if Ray were in the room with us. Why was I kidding myself, he *was* here, reaching out to touch me again.

"You confronted Slaight about the photos?" Dad spoke suddenly, fiercely.

"Yes. He . . . confessed, you could say."

"Confessed?" Dad repeated, glancing at me.

Stephens sighed. "He 'confessed' to having a sexual

relationship with Jeff. Period. No force. No kidnapping."

I would have given anything not to laugh then, but I did, a short, sharp bark that sounded more like a cough.

Stephens ignored me. "Slaight says Jeff was hitchhiking when he picked him up. He says the kid asked to stay with him, and anything that happened after that was mutual."

"That's . . . ridiculous," Dad sputtered after another long silence. "He can't expect anyone to believe him."

"He does," Stephens said. "That's his case."

"But . . . " Dad looked to me for help. I said nothing.

"It's past time for Jeff to give his side," Stephens said, "and give it strong."

" 'His side?' " Dad's voice was hushed. " 'His *side?*' "

"Sorry," Stephens said briskly. "Bad choice of words. But true all the same."

The three of us sat in tense silence until Dad reached over and gently clasped the back of my neck. All I could feel was Ray's hand doing the same thing.

"Don't touch me," I said, shaking him off, gooseflesh covering my arms.

"Sorry," Dad said quickly. I sat on the edge of the chair, wringing my hands together, one leg vibrating from nervousness.

"I can't do this," I said, hearing the echo of all the other times I had retreated from the truth.

"Slaight is talking about you," Stephens said deliberately. "The one thing he won't say is where he kept you. He says you were on the road mostly. Driving. Camping. For two and a half years? Hard to believe."

I did not respond.

"What is he trying to hide, Jeff? What are you?" I looked up at him quickly. Stephens's eyes narrowed. "What are you afraid we're going to find there? More pictures? Videotapes?"

Pain spiked through my stomach and I gasped. He nodded to himself, as if he already knew. "You know that anything like that—anything linking Slaight with you—is just more evidence against him."

"You're wrong," I said fiercely, the pain strengthening my voice. "You're making stuff up . . . throwing it out . . . trying to catch me."

"We need your help," Stephens said. "You need to help yourself."

I squirmed, wanting to be gone. "He kidnapped me. I told you about that. I'll say it in court."

"It's not enough. What are you going to do when Slaight's lawyer asks you about the sex?"

Dad held up one hand. "Wait. Just wait. He isn't going to ask Jeff about that."

"Ken . . . " Stephens shook his head. "You don't understand. That's part of their strategy. Slaight and his lawyer know Jeff isn't talking, they know he's scared—"

"I'm not scared," I said. Neither of them looked at me.

"Jeff isn't talking," Stephens repeated. "And they know it. That gives Slaight the freedom to shape the story any way he wants. He's *admitting* that he had something going with the kid. He's not ashamed of it."

"Shut up," I said softly.

"Slaight says the pictures were your idea, Jeff. He says you offered to pose for them one Christmas."

Sickened, I felt my throat go dry. All I could do was shake my head.

"You gonna let that stand?" Stephens persisted. "You gonna let Ray Slaight do your talking for you?"

Dad held up his hand. "Enough. What do you need from Jeff? Today."

"The location where he was kept," Stephens said promptly.

"No," I said before he finished speaking. "No."

Moving deliberately this time, Stephens reached over and grasped my wrist. I stared down at his meaty hand, then back at his face.

"He's still got you, Jeff. He's a hundred and fifty miles away and he's still holding you down. When are you going to fight back?"

I pulled my wrist away, glaring at him. "I did fight back. And guess what? *It didn't work.*"

"Okay," Stephens said. "You fought back. Tell me about that. One incident."

I stared at him blankly. The punchline of every incident with Ray was the same: I lost. And every loss had pulled me deeper into his world. I could taste that defeat even now, sitting in the quiet living room with Stephens and Dad.

I opened my mouth to reply to Stephens, not sure what I was going to say, but Dad spoke for me.

"Give him some time to think about this," he said. "A few more days . . . "

Never.

I DRAGGED THE RAKE ACROSS THE FROST-hardened ground, bringing with it only a few of the thumb-sized oak leaves that covered the front lawn. Grumbling to myself, I tried again, this time applying more force. A half hour's work so far had produced only a modest pile of leaves and a growing ache in my back and forearms. I had no energy for the job, and my heart wasn't in it. But I knew why I was out there. The finished product—a clean lawn, the leaves neatly bagged and stored out of sight—would serve as both an offering and an apology to Dad.

Look, Daddy, I raked the lawn for you. See? See what a good boy I am?

I curled my lip, disgusted with myself. As if anything could be good enough for him now. Holding the rake for support, I rested, staring at the ground.

"Jeff!" I looked up quickly. Vin was striding toward me across the vacant lot, moving with purpose.

"Shit," I said under my breath, starting to rake again as if *I* had a purpose.

"Hey," he said as he reached me, an edge of aggression in his voice.

He knows.

"Hi," I said calmly, bluffing it out. "You're early. It can't be lunch yet."

Vin shook his head impatiently. "It's break time," he said, looking back over his shoulder.

"Huh." I moved away from him, attacking a clump of wet leaves stuck to the side of the house.

Vin came around and grabbed the rake out of my hands. Shocked, I stepped back from him.

"Is it true?" he said, staring at me.

I couldn't meet his eyes. "Is what true?"

Vin tossed the rake to one side. "There's a story in the Modesto *Bee* today. My mom showed it to me at breakfast. It says that guy took naked pictures of you. That's what those reporters were asking about, isn't it?"

I shrugged, chilled, wanting away from him but afraid to move.

"Hey, *I'm* in that goddamn story," Vin said, his voice low and furious. "A picture of me, anyway, standing next to you outside your house. That went over big today."

"What do you want me to say, Vin?"

"Why did you lie? Why didn't you even give me the chance to handle it?"

At this I looked up. Vin was squinting at me, his head tilted. There was a softness in his expression, a quality of hurt—he was giving me an opening.

I would not—could not—take it. "I don't know what you're talking about. I didn't lie to you about anything."

"You said he never touched you!" Vin was angry again. He took a step forward, his hands clenched by his sides. "You told me that and I went with it. That's what I've been telling people. That's how I've been defending you."

"You've been *defending* me, huh?" My voice was shaking. "Defending me against what?"

Vin gave me a "come on!" tilt of his head. "You know what."

"Uh-huh," I said after a moment, nodding. "Well, now you can stop defending me. You have my permission, if you need it." I could feel my defensive energy starting to drain away. Stepping around him carefully, averting my eyes as I passed, I headed back toward the porch steps.

"Jeff, wait," Vin called after me, not following.

Halfway up the steps, I turned back to him, keeping a solid grasp on the porch rail. "What?" I said, my voice weary.

"You lied to me," Vin said, faltering for the first time. "You sent me out to fight your battles, and you didn't . . . you didn't give me the ammunition."

"*Ammunition?*" I watched his face redden but Vin did not look away. "Hey, no one sent you anywhere to do anything."

"You hung me out to dry," he said stubbornly. "You don't know what they're saying."

I considered him. "Fuck them. And fuck you. Anyway, you're off the case. So forget about it."

"It is true, isn't it," he said, softly this time. "You were makin' it with that guy."

"I have to go inside now," I told him, fighting to keep my voice steady. "See you in school."

"*School?*" I heard the concern in Vin's voice, still there even amidst his anger and disgust at me. "Jeff, forget about school."

I let myself into the house, closing the door behind me. I did not look back.

The Wayne *Telegraph* arrived at four. Its banner headline read *Police Find Nude Photos of Local Kidnap Victim.* I knew Vin would not be happy to find himself on the front page with me again. Maybe the suspicious frown the photographer had caught would set Vin right again in his friends' eyes.

I turned the television on after that, scanning back and forth among the four Sacramento stations that considered Wayne part of their region. I kept missing the promos for their local news programs coming up at five. I cursed Charlie to her face when she tried to distract me, and after that, she left me alone.

At five o'clock, it was as I had feared, but not believed possible. Each station led off with the news about the pictures. I flipped back and forth until the story was played out. When I turned to leave the room, I found Connie and Brian standing in the archway, watching along with me.

Dad was home by six, furious—at the media, he said. I avoided him, knowing that part of his anger, whether he admitted it or not, was intended for me.

"There was no reason they had to go public with this," he raged at the dinner table. "They're playing right into Slaight's hands." He cut Connie off as she started to speak. "What? Don't tell me to relax. These people have no understanding—"

With difficulty, Connie broke in. "I wasn't going to say that, Ken. I was going to say that I don't think we need to discuss this anymore. Especially in front of the kids. The story's out, and we all feel bad about it. Why go over it again?"

I looked at Connie with approval. That even quieted Dad.

"Jeff?" Brian's voice was wary. Dad looked up at him quickly.

"Yes?" I said uninvitingly.

"That guy—" he started.

Dad jumped in immediately. "Brian, listen to your mother. We're not going to talk about this."

"But I just want to say something to Jeff," he protested.

"Brian," Connie warned softly.

He waited, then blurted out, "I'm sorry that guy made you do stuff, Jeff. That's all I want to say."

I waited for Dad to jump on him again. He didn't. The silence lengthened.

Ray didn't do anything to me. Yeah, I took my

clothes off for him, and yeah, he took pictures of me, but that doesn't mean . . .

Without looking at any of them, I mumbled, "Sorry I lied to you guys."

After a short silence, Charlie leaned over and kissed me on the cheek. I stared down at my plate, ashamed.

"It's okay," she said quietly, resting her head against mine for a moment.

"So," Dad said, clearing his throat, "Jeff, about tomorrow . . ."

I had an appointment the next day at Wayne High to register and sign up for classes.

"Yes?" I said, wary of any more changes, any more "news."

"I'm going over with you. I decided to take a day off work."

"Why?" I said quickly. "I can do it myself."

Why do it at all? You know what's going to happen.

But I would not explain that to Dad, or ask for quarter, or make myself any more pathetic than he already thought me.

"Dad," Charlie said, "are you sure . . . I mean . . . "

"What is it, Charlie?" Dad asked, his tone kinder than usual.

"Well . . . " She glanced at me. "Maybe you should wait a little bit longer before Jeff goes back to school. People were talking about him today. You know, because of what was in the papers and stuff."

Dad sighed, putting his water glass down. "How long

do we wait? Two weeks? Two months? There's no guarantee things will be any easier then. Jeff, as tough as this may be, I don't see any percentage in waiting. We can't let that man take away any more of your opportunities."

"Okay, Dad," I said, to stop him. "I'm going. I am. I just think I should sign up for classes myself, like we planned." I couldn't tell him the truth, that I was afraid of what he might hear about me if we went over together.

Dad looked a little hurt. "Are you meeting Vin over there? Is that it?"

"No," I said flatly. Charlie stared at me.

"Jeff, I'm coming with you tomorrow," Dad said. "You'll have plenty of time for independence when you start school for real on Monday."

I was silent during the short ride to school the next day.

"Nervous?" Dad asked as we reached Wayne High.

"A little," I mumbled, sinking down lower in the seat. Hordes of students filled the sidewalk in front of the high school. Another mob was crossing Delano Road, the public street that split the science, shop and agriculture complexes off from the rest of the campus. Dad turned right off Delano into the Wayne High faculty and visitors parking lot.

"Isn't that Vin?" he asked, cruising slowly through the lot, pointing up toward the redbrick science building. "Over there, coming out of that classroom?"

"I don't know," I said, staring down at my hands.

"Well, look up so you will know." Dad sounded impatient.

Vin was alone, a backpack slung carelessly across his shoulder. He called out to someone in the parking lot, looking past the Jeep, apparently not seeing us. "Yeah, that's him," I said.

Keep driving, I begged silently, but Dad pulled into a spot next to the short flight of stairs Vin was descending. I kept my head down, making no move to leave the Jeep, but Dad stepped out quickly and intercepted him.

"How are you, Vin?" Dad asked, motioning to me. I opened the door slowly and took my time getting out.

"I'm okay, Mr. Hart," Vin said, with a noticeable lack of enthusiasm, shifting his backpack to the other side.

"Perini!" someone called from the lot. Vin brightened, waving in the direction of the voice.

"Well, I better get—"

"Jeff's signing up for classes today," Dad broke in. I stood behind him, staring at my feet.

"Yeah? That's good. Well, I have to get going. See you, Jeff. See you, Mr. Hart." Vin took off at a faster pace than his usual swagger.

"What's wrong with him?" Dad sounded bewildered.

"He knows about the pictures," I said simply.

"I can't believe it," Dad said with some bitterness. "I thought that kid was your friend."

The counselor was a woman who didn't look much older than me. It was easy for Dad to convince her that I should be placed in college prep classes. As she ran down my schedule—PE, composition, algebra, U.S. history, biology, and computer science—I felt my stomach fluttering. I looked forward to the distraction the homework would provide, but I still didn't see how I could jump from being an eighth-grade dropout to a high school junior preparing to attend university.

Afterward, Dad took me downtown to a Mexican restaurant for lunch. After the waitress had taken our orders, he said hesitantly, "Jeff, the PE thing, how are you going to handle that?"

It was the first time he had mentioned my back since the day I had told him about it.

I took a deep breath. "When I change, I'm going to wear an undershirt. And I won't shower."

"School is the best thing for you, Jeff." Dad sounded like he was trying to convince himself. "I'm sorry about Vin. I had him factored in as someone who would help you."

"I don't need help," I said, stung. "I don't need him. I'm not going to school for friends, anyway. I'm going to learn stuff and get good grades and . . . all that." Dad nodded, looking unhappy.

We were quiet as the waitress dropped off our Cokes. Then Dad said, "I've scheduled you for a doctor's appointment next Friday. Someone from the DA's office in San Francisco is coming up with a police photographer. They'll meet us at the doctor's office. The

DA needs the preliminary medical report and pictures of your back as evidence."

The good news was piling up. "I feel fine," I said, taking a sip of my drink. I saw that my hands were shaking, and set the glass down fast.

"Is the doctor a man or woman?" The words were out of my mouth before I realized the implications of my question. Blushing, I reached for a tortilla chip.

"It's Dr. Torrence. Remember him?"

I recalled a heavy, middle-aged man who barely spoke. "Yeah, I remember him. But I'm fine. I don't need any doctor."

"*I* need you to go to the doctor then," Dad said. "I need to know, for my peace of mind, for yours . . . that you're all right."

"Dad," I said softly, "please don't talk about this stuff."

"The DA's office is trying to get a court order to test him, but so far—"

"You're talking about AIDS, aren't you?"

Now Dad's face was red. "I . . . yes."

"I'm okay," I said with more assurance than I felt.

"I know you are," Dad said quickly. "But you're going to be tested anyway. Not just for that. You need a complete physical exam. I should have done it sooner."

"Fine, whatever," I said. "Excuse me, okay?" Dad nodded and I slid out of the booth quickly, avoiding his eyes.

Locking the bathroom door, I stared at myself in the mirror that wrapped around three-quarters of the octagonal room.

I looked awful. My eyes were reddened and moist, though I didn't feel like crying at all. My hair was growing out from the semi-crewcut Mel had given me, and it stuck up at funny angles. My hands were shoved deep into the pockets of jeans that bagged around my waist. Worst of all, my face was bright red.

God, how can he stand to look at me?

Had I looked this way at the high school?

Sure you did. You were just as embarrassed there, weren't you?

No, this was worse, because there I hadn't known that Dad was discussing the possibility I had AIDS with . . . who? The district attorney's office, Stephens, of course. Ray.

And how do you get AIDS, Dad?

"I can't stand this," I said quietly.

Someone tapped at the door. "Jeff?" Dad said. "Jeff, are you in there? Are you all right?"

I closed my eyes.

Leave me alone, Dad. Leave me alone.

I couldn't sleep at all the night before school started. Around four I gave it up as impossible and turned my light on. My heart was pounding against my chest, too hard for me to ignore.

God, what am I going to do?

I stood in the hallway, grateful for the light Dad left on every night, for me I knew.

Sixteen years old and you need a night-light. No, you need the whole hallway lit up, don't you? Pathetic.

Charlie's door was shut, as usual. Down the hall from me, one door over from the bathroom, Brian's door was ajar, and I could hear his quick, shallow breathing.

You're going to do it anyway, so just do it.

I walked to the end of the hallway, stopping at the room near the top of the stairs. Leaning my head against the wall, I waited until I heard Dad's deep, steady, even breathing. Connie slept so quietly I could never hear her, but she wasn't the one I needed.

I sank back against the wall next to their door, suddenly sleepy. I sat like that for a moment, then stretched out along the carpeted hallway, resting my head on my arms.

"Jeff?"

I opened my eyes slowly, not knowing if I had slept for minutes or hours. I was curled up on the floor, my arms straight down in front of me, my cheek pressed against the carpet. Brian was crouched alongside me.

He looked concerned, his brown hair falling over his eyes the same way Dad's did. I should have been embarrassed, but I wasn't. I smiled at him.

"Hey."

"Did you have a nightmare?" he asked, his voice strangely mature.

"No. I just couldn't stay in my room anymore."

"Why?"

"Because I was afraid," I said flatly. Brian nodded. He glanced into Dad and Connie's room, then leaned forward.

"You can sleep in my room, if you want," he said quietly.

"No," I said too quickly, raising myself on one elbow. His face fell. "I mean, thanks, but that's probably not a good idea." Unbidden, a quick image of Brian and me curled up on the same bed flashed through my mind, and Connie discovering us that way.

For the first time I felt a flash of pure hatred at Ray. *Goddamn you for spoiling everything.*

Brian had recovered, his face set now in a kind of loving concern too old for his years. "I could stay here until you fall asleep again," he said. "Would that be okay?"

I waited a moment, then let myself relax, sliding back down onto the carpet, resting my head on my outstretched arm. "Okay," I mumbled, closing my eyes.

I awoke to the sound of Dad's alarm and his muffled groan as he shut it off. Brian was gone. I crept back to my room, falling into bed and burrowing under the covers.

Two hours after that, Charlie woke me for school. I felt like I'd slept about ten minutes.

Charlie glanced over at me as we were leaving the house. "You look good, Jeff," she offered shyly.

I smiled wryly, my looks not being the main thing on my mind. "You're the one who looks good," I tossed back, then realized it was true. Charlie wore a green sweater and black pants, and her hair was pulled tightly back in a braid.

As soon as we left the subdivision, I saw the first groups of students, some of them heading to the high school like we were, others standing around in groups of four or five, smoking and talking.

"We should leave earlier tomorrow," Charlie murmured.

But no one took any particular notice of us as we joined the stream. Charlie was walking too fast, a few steps ahead of me, books clutched to her chest, her head down.

"Charlie," I said quietly, reaching out to touch her elbow. She slowed immediately, giving me an apologetic smile. No need to advertise our position.

"Okay," Charlie said as we walked along in step. "We both have PE first period, that's in the gym. You have English with Tower after that, right?" I nodded. "Okay. After PE, wait for me by the fence next to the baseball field, and I'll walk you to class."

I caught sight of Vin's truck parked in the student lot where it had been the day he, Brian and I had come to the high school to play basketball. My mood soured as I realized I would almost certainly run into him today.

"Jeff? Is that okay, if we meet after PE?"

"Hey, I can find my own way around," I snapped, glancing over at her. Charlie was looking down again, frowning, holding her books to herself in a gesture that looked more like one of comfort than protection.

"Sorry," I said awkwardly. "Sure, we can meet after PE, if you want."

Charlie smiled at me. "We might have PE together, anyway. The coaches combine the boys' and girls' classes a lot, for volleyball and badminton and things."

As we entered the open courtyard between the computer building and the Humanities complex, I began to feel stares coming our way and picked out the sound of my name spoken by many different voices. By instinct I kept walking, staring straight ahead, but I could feel my heart beating faster. Charlie walked beside me, her presence delicate but steady. Then I heard it, just a whisper, but the word hit me like a fist.

"Fag." I couldn't stop myself from looking around to find the source. To our right, by a water fountain, three boys who had to be freshmen laughed together. One of them, slight and scrawny with a patchy mustache, saw me looking and said it louder. "Fag!"

Charlie squeezed my arm. "Ignore them, Jeff. They're losers." I shook her off, walking faster, Charlie scrambling to keep up.

"Sorry," I muttered after a moment, slowing my pace. She nodded tightly, not looking at me.

"Hi, Jeff," a group of girls screamed in unison from the outside railing of the classroom building above us. I jumped, managing a halfhearted wave in their direction. They laughed at that, talking excitedly with one another. While their laughter sounded friendly, I was chilled through.

"Where's Sherry?" Charlie muttered, stopping abruptly. "She was supposed to meet us by the Humanities building. Do you see her anywhere?" She looked around, glaring at anyone who caught her eye.

"Charlie, relax." I saw that she was trembling, and I was able to forget myself. "C'mon. We'll catch up with Sherry later."

"Okay, Jeff." She took a deep breath and we began walking again. Two guys brushed by us, headed the opposite direction. After they passed, I heard one say, "That's that guy." The other replied, "*Him?* No way."

The first one muttered something I could not hear and then they laughed together, explosively.

"I hate them," Charlie whispered, but neither of us looked back.

The path we walked ran parallel to the football and baseball fields, and I looked at them with longing and regret. If I had never met Ray Slaight, I would have been in my third year of playing, possibly starring, in both sports for Wayne High. Vin would have been my teammate and best friend. At sixteen, I might have had a few casual girlfriends already, maybe even a serious one. The kids at Wayne High would know me only as an athlete, a good student, a person secure in a tight circle of friends.

But because I had been in the right place at the wrong time, I was a curiosity, a freak, someone worthy of, at best, pity.

It's not fair, you idiots. What happened to me could have happened to any of you. It could have been any one of you, and if it was, I wouldn't be treating you this way.

The rage that swept through me then was enough to carry me the rest of the way to the gym stiff-backed and head up.

Charlie and I split off and I headed over to the boys' locker room. I slowed down, sweat breaking out on my forehead as I saw Vin huddled with Andy Keller and two other guys under the awning next to the locker-room door. My first thought was of flight, damn everything else. But one of them had seen me, a squat fireplug of a guy I recognized as Ryan Tanner, one of our group from Wayne Elementary.

"Hey, there he is," Ryan said, nudging Andy. Vin looked around quickly, then turned back, shaking his head slightly.

"Shee . . . it," Andy drawled, staring at me, his lip curling. Ryan laughed. I had enough of that and pushed open the door to the locker room.

It was crowded and noisy inside, and lots of guys were already dressed out. I stopped just inside the door, panicked already by the hot, close smell of the room and the proximity of so many of my peers. Why had Dad sent me here? None of his pious prescriptions made sense to me now. My heart racing, I remembered the four behind me, and stepped aside just as they burst through the door.

I couldn't stop myself from looking over at them. Vin met my eyes, his expression unreadable. I turned away fast, almost tripping over my own feet, reaching out for a locker to brace myself.

"Hey!" some kid yelled right in my ear, and I jumped back, mumbling an apology. The locker was his, apparently.

"Watch out, Foster, he's looking at you," the guy next to him said, grinning.

"Get out of the way, why don't you?" Foster said, glaring at me.

"Sorry," I said again, then flushed, hating my own weakness. I stepped back into the narrow aisle between the rows of lockers and the shower area—then stopped, paralyzed, as I saw the group coming through. Ryan and the other guy pushed past me, snickering, then Vin, his eyes averted. Andy was last. He motored to a stop in front of me, so close I could smell his breath. The rough tiles of the shower wall crunched against my back.

"What?" I tried, shrugging, daring to meet his eyes.

He sneered, shaking his head. "You make me sick, man."

"Yeah?" I said, proud of the calmness of my voice.

"Let some guy take pictures of you." I looked down. When Andy spoke again, his voice was stronger. "Yeah, you and that guy."

"Andy, come on," Vin said from somewhere nearby. He sounded tired. I didn't bother to look up.

Andy waited a moment, letting me feel it, then drew back, snorting, walking away with a swagger.

I sighed involuntarily, leaning back against the tiled wall, standing up again when I noticed a short, muscular man, unmistakably a coach, headed in my direction.

"Jeff Hart?" I nodded. "I'm Jake Lewis." He held out his hand, and after a moment, I took it. Lewis's handshake was firm and brief. "Come up to the office and I'll give you your locker assignment."

I was wary, expecting questions or a lecture or both, but Lewis was businesslike as he laid out the rules and routine of his PE class. The only personal remark he made was to let me know that he coached track in addition to teaching PE. After urging me to try out for the team in spring, Lewis handed me a lock, combination attached, and pointed the way to locker 105.

My locker was located in an alcove, off from the crowded main section of the room. Whether I had been given that location by accident or design, I was thankful. The two guys dressing near my locker didn't even look up at me.

Still, I waited for them to finish. I opened the locker slowly and put my backpack inside. Sitting down on the bench, I untied the pack and pulled out the green shorts and T-shirt uniform I was supposed to wear.

In seconds, the locker room went from pandemonium to near silence as the bulk of the class followed Coach Lewis through the passageway to the gym.

Five minutes passed. I knew I could not put it off any longer. I dressed out, feeling cold and exposed.

Badminton nets were strung across the gym floor, and eight separate courts had been set up. Coach Lewis and a tall, blond woman dressed in sweats were lecturing a mix of guys and girls standing over by the basketball bleachers. I joined the edge of the circle. Charlie stood opposite, near the coaches. She caught my eye and smiled over at me. I nodded, giving her a half wave.

"Okay, people," the woman teacher concluded, "break into small groups and practice serving."

Charlie hurried over. "Sherry's going to get the racquets. Practice with us, okay?" Her smile looked forced, and I wondered what she had heard while I was in the locker room.

I hadn't played badminton since I was about nine, but the knack returned to me quickly. Soon Charlie and Sherry were giggling and I was trying hard not to smile as we became involved in an elaborate game of hot potato.

Sherry let the birdie drop when Coach Lewis blew his whistle. "Listen up. Break into teams of four, boys against girls, extra people rotate in. Come on, let's get some games going."

Charlie and Sherry looked at each other. That my dilemma was as obvious to them as it was to me was humiliating.

"Maybe you can stay with us, Jeff . . . " Sherry said, trailing off.

I closed my eyes a moment, then smiled at her. "Nah. Don't worry about it."

"Hey, Sherry, play with us," a girl called from a nearby court. "You too, Charlie." Sherry moved off, but Charlie hesitated, looking back at me.

"Go ahead," I said, trying not to sound impatient. Charlie nodded, walking off. I stood back, trying to blend into the wall.

Vin's team was playing fast and furious already, lined up against four girls who looked like athletes themselves. I watched them for a while until I noticed Andy watching *me*. I looked away fast, catching the coach's eye as I did.

"Hart, what are you doing over there?" he called, coming my way. Blushing, I shrugged my shoulders. "Find a team then and . . . " He hesitated, looking around. "There!" he said, pointing to the nearest court: Charlie's. "Stand by the net and wait your turn to rotate in."

"Yes sir," I said automatically, blushing again as he turned to stare.

"Right, then," Lewis nodded awkwardly, showing me the way.

"Aw no, Coach," one of the guys cried as I arrived. "Why do *we* have to take him?"

As I shuffled in place, Lewis watched the guy, who wilted under his stare. Lewis turned back to me. "Got a watch? Good. Let them go another five minutes, then rotate in. Hooten"—he pointed—"you're out at that point."

"Coach, why don't you put Hart on the girls' side?" Another guy spoke, grinning, looking over at Hooten for approval.

Lewis stared at him. "Now why should I do that, Woods?"

"*You* know, Coach. You're the one who told us . . . "

I closed my eyes. It seemed another group of people had been discussing me and my problems.

"You're out, Woods," Lewis said coldly.

"Come with me." Lewis strode off toward the far corner of the gym, Woods trailing after him sullenly. Hooten watched them go, grinning, then started the game again, serving brutally hard into a girl's face. I stayed where the coach had indicated, trying to look cool but shaking inside. Glancing at my watch again, I saw that the period wasn't even half over.

I wasn't about to insist on rotating into the game,

but Sherry, who seemed to have appointed herself captain, did it for me.

"Okay, Mark, it's been five minutes. Let Jeff take your place."

Hooten said, "No way," just as I said, "That's okay. I'll just watch." I regarded him coolly. He stared at me, smiling. I had backed down too easily.

Steeling myself, I looked him over. Hooten's mouth appeared to be the strongest thing about him. He was easily five inches shorter than me, and a potbelly strained against the fabric of his T-shirt. I looked him over again, sneering this time, wanting him to know that if I cared to do it, I could best him physically, no problem.

For the first time, Hooten looked uncertain. But he blustered it out. "Don't look at me, boy. You *faggot.*"

I blushed again, retreating. How could a word hold so much power over me? A word, after everything I lived through with Ray.

"You can have your fucking game," I muttered, turning my back on him, heading for the gym wall.

"So, Hart, did you like it?" Hooten called after me. I stopped, my face burning. Charlie came over, and touched my arm. I recognized the expression on her face.

"Charlie, don't." I meant both for her not to cry and not to touch me. She understood, backing away.

I could think of nothing to say to Hooten. But I knew, at least, I could face him down. Turning back, I met his stare directly, keeping my face expressionless. Hooten grinned, knowing he had the edge.

Vin's team stood motionless, watching the action on our court. Vin was at the edge of the group, his eyes on Hooten, head cocked to listen. I felt like a deer stunned by the headlights. I knew disaster was coming and there was absolutely nothing I could do to prevent it.

"So, *sweet* Hart, you miss getting it regular?" Hooten laughed, glancing around at the others. He stopped laughing when he saw Vin coming his way.

Swearing to myself, I scanned the room for Coach Lewis. He was at the other end of the gym talking to Woods, writing something down on a clipboard. I didn't want this. I didn't want any of it.

Vin walked right into Hooten's comfort zone, towering over him. When Hooten tried to back up, Vin grabbed a handful of T-shirt, pulling him close.

"You know what they say, Hooten. The more a guy talks about it, the more likely he is one." Hooten was actually standing on tiptoes.

"I wasn't talking to you," he choked out, trying to backpedal. Vin's friends, including Andy, came to stand behind him.

"No, but I'm talking to *you*, dickhead," Vin said calmly.

"Stop it," I told him. "I can fight my own battles."

Vin considered that, then said, "I don't like assholes, so this is my battle." He focused his attention back on Hooten. "You don't say a word to him without saying it to me first. Then I'll let you know if it's okay. Got that?"

Vin kept his hold on Hooten until he nodded. Then he released him like he was throwing away a used tissue. The girls and most of the guys laughed as Hooten stumbled, then fell to the floor.

Coach Lewis charged over, ready to explode. He looked from Hooten, still on the floor, to Vin, cool and collected a few feet away from him.

"Looks like I'm going to have to baby-sit these boys, Perini," he said finally.

"Yes sir," Vin said blandly. "Coach, I want Hart on my team."

Lewis regarded me. "Yeah, go ahead," he said crisply, nodding to Vin. "And Hooten, get off your ass unless you want to join Woods and take an F for the day."

We reassembled in Vin's court. "Hey, Keller," he said to Andy, "let Jeff take your spot." Andy looked at him in disbelief. Vin stared back at him, raising his eyebrows. Andy gave, muttering to himself. I stepped into Andy's spot, holding my breath as I passed him.

I was the first one out of the gym when the bell rang. The guys filing into the locker room after me were mostly subdued. But each one, as he passed, glanced over at me, and I heard several of them rehashing what had happened between Vin and Hooten, embellishments added.

No matter what Dad expected from me, I had had

enough. It was not in me to serve as chief freak in a traveling sideshow. Vin's gesture was meaningless, stemming from sudden pity or the urge to play big man for an audience. I couldn't accept it either way.

I paced outside the girls' locker room, waiting for Charlie so I could tell her I was leaving. My foot caught on a depression in the sidewalk and I stumbled into a chain link fence, cursing. But I felt how the sun had touched the metal, and I threaded my fingers through the links, leaning back, gradually resting my entire weight against the fence.

After a minute or two, I heard the distinctive creak of the boys' locker room door swinging open, and then someone calling my name. I stood up, tense. Vin came charging around the corner. When he saw me, he stopped dead.

"Why'd you run out like that?" he said, attempting a smile. I gave him the coldest, most knowing look I could muster. "Come on, say something."

"Okay. Thanks. Is that what you want to hear? You're free. You can feel good about yourself now."

Vin stared at me, tilting his head as if he had not heard correctly. "What are you talking about?"

"I'm impressed, the coach was impressed, the geek was impressed. No one's watching now. I'll take it from here."

"What does that mean, you'll take it from here?" Vin was starting to look angry.

Charlie came out of the girls' locker room and hurried over to join us.

"Charlie, don't worry about anything, but I'm leaving." I left without waiting for her response.

"Hey," Vin called, "I'm not done talking to you."

"Let it go," I said, loudly enough so he would catch it, repeating the words to myself.

Let it go.

As I walked away from them, I could still feel the cross-hatching of the fence against my back.

VIN CAME POUNDING AFTER ME BEFORE I HAD even reached the end of the Humanities building.

"What's the point," I muttered, but slowed down. Some of the classroom doors were open and the last thing I wanted was to explain to some teacher who I was and where I was going. Vin caught up to me and we walked along together in silence.

When we were past the building, out in the open courtyard, I stopped, turning to face him.

"Look," I said, choosing my words carefully, "whatever you think you're doing now, you don't need to. I forgive you, if that's what you want. I even understand. I'm embarrassed to be me, so why shouldn't you be embarrassed to be around me?"

Vin looked down.

"Maybe you weren't trying to show off in the gym. Maybe you really were being a nice guy. But what is that worth? Right before that you and Andy and those guys were laughing at me. They must have been saying the same kind of things Hooten was."

"I never laughed at you. You have to believe that. I

just stood there while they . . . " Vin hesitated. "I just stood there."

I watched him for a moment, then sighed. The bell rang, and the surrounding classrooms began to empty out. "Just forget it, okay? See you around."

But Vin kept pace with me as I retraced the route Charlie and I had taken that morning. When we reached the student parking lot, he stepped in front of me, blocking my path. I looked at him in disbelief, wondering how far he was prepared to take this.

"Don't leave now. It'll look terrible. Come on. Let me walk you to your next class."

I laughed sharply. "You and Charlie. I must really be pathetic."

Vin squinted at me, frowning. "What's does that mean?"

"You want to lead me around campus? Like your goddamn puppy?"

He didn't flinch. "You'll need help at first. Once people know you're with me and they know I'm okay with it, they'll treat you right. You saw what happened in the gym."

"Big man," I said softly.

"I am if I want to be," he said, not sounding offended.

"An hour ago you didn't want anything to do with me. What's different now?"

"Jeff, come on," he said quietly. "I made a mistake, all right? Let me make it up to you. Please."

I searched Vin's face, really looking at him for the

first time since I had come home. Suddenly I saw the boy I had known so well, so long ago. We had been inseparable once. From fifth grade through eighth, barely a day had gone by without our seeing each other. But what did a childhood friendship mean now? What *could* it mean, after everything, after Ray? Ray had stolen that from me too, I realized: the ability to have a friend.

"Sorry, Vin," I muttered, my voice thick. "I . . . "

"Come on," he said quietly, but insistently. "Let's take a ride."

Not sure why I was doing it, I climbed into Vin's truck. It was only then I realized how tired I was. It seemed as if I had been standing forever. My legs shook in delayed reaction. I clasped my thighs to control the effect, but Vin didn't appear to notice.

We headed out of Wayne onto a series of backcountry roads. I began to recognize the landscape, small, hilly farms and ranches. When we passed a sign advertising the turnoff for Mark Twain's cabin, I knew we would soon reach the bridge over New Melones Reservoir, the dividing line between Tuolumne and Calaveras counties. Before the bridge, though, Vin turned off, taking a left so sharp for a breathless second I thought we were on two wheels.

Still speeding, Vin headed down a narrow road lined on either side with bushes and oak trees. I caught a glimpse of Melones Reservoir as we swerved around a corner.

"Okay, I give up. Where are we going?"

Vin took his time answering. "Down to the reservoir."

After we passed two picnic areas, Vin turned down another road that declined steeply. The whole reservoir was visible now, looking gray in the cold sunlight. I saw that the road we were on eventually turned into a boat launch. Just before it did, Vin veered left, into an empty parking lot the size of four football fields put together. The lake spread out before us, and I could see the green hills of Calaveras County across the water.

It was dead silent once Vin turned the truck off. I didn't see or hear any signs of life, not even birds.

"You come here a lot?" I said quietly, knowing suddenly that he did.

"Yeah, I guess." Vin looked sheepish. "We come out here to drink. After hours. Me and the guys."

I nodded. "The guys."

"I come out here by myself sometimes too. It's a good place to be alone."

"So why are we here, Vin?"

"Because I'm sorry." Vin clenched his fists and stared at them. "I just have this feeling if you walk off I'm not going to see you again."

I closed my eyes in sudden pain, tears pricking at my eyelids. Damn him.

When I trusted myself to speak, I reached for anger. "I'd think you'd be glad about not seeing me again." Vin looked at me quickly. "What do you think school's going to be like tomorrow? For you, I mean. Someone might have seen you leaving with me. And what happened in the gym, they'll be talking about that."

"So what," Vin said, angry himself. "I'm your friend, and I'm not ashamed of that."

"Not anymore, you mean." I stared at him.

"Right," he said, unflinching. "I was ashamed before. Embarrassed. All that. Jeff, you put me in a hell of a spot. You made me look like an asshole in front of those guys. You had your reasons, I know, I know." Vin raised his voice as I tried to respond. "But if you had told me the truth from day one, I could have found a way to tell them and make it right before they even saw you again."

I shook my head. "I can't believe that you would have known what to do if I said, 'Yeah, Ray molested me,' that day on the bleachers. Come on, Vin. You would have wanted *out*, and fast."

"You don't know that," Vin said, but he looked away. "You should have given me the chance . . . "

"Maybe," I conceded, not believing him. "But God, Vin, I can't . . . I can't think about it myself. . . . "

You don't think about anything else.

"I can't talk about it with my dad, with anyone, and you expected me to tell you? Why? Just because you asked?"

"We were friends," Vin mumbled, looking at his hands.

"Right. We were friends. Three years ago."

Vin did not respond.

I shifted on the hard seat, restless. "I knew I wasn't ready for all this. But my dad . . . all this stuff, school, friends, *you*." Vin flinched. "This is his idea, and I'm not goddamn ready. You're right, I should have warned you off. That night you called, Christmas, I should have told you then to stay away from me. That's what I wanted to do, but I didn't know how to say it. I was afraid, I guess."

Vin glanced over, tossing his hair out of his eyes. "You were afraid of me?"

Were?

"Yeah." He didn't respond and I was freshly embarrassed. "This is stupid, Vin. Let's go back now."

"Why were you afraid of me?"

I sighed, shaking my head.

"You mean you were afraid to tell me, right? About you and that guy. Okay, I can see that."

As much as I wanted out of the conversation, I had to respond to that. "You don't know what you're talking about," I said softly. "You have no idea what it was like. And you sound like an idiot pretending you do."

He looked at me swiftly. "Hey . . . "

"What do you think happened between me and 'that guy'? Some big romance?"

"Jeff . . . " Vin shifted, looking uncomfortable.

"No," I said. "What do you think you're trying to tolerate here?"

"I don't know what you mean."

"He kidnapped me." I spoke the words flatly but

inside I wondered if Stephens was right, if Ray's story would be the one people believed.

"I don't think you did anything wrong, Jeff." Vin watched me solemnly until I met his eyes, absurdly grateful, trying not to show it. "Let me try to explain, okay?"

"You've got the keys," I said coldly.

He nodded once. "Andy, Ryan, all of them—those guys are not my friends. I stand around with them before school and during lunch. We cut each other down, rank each other out, and tell dumb jokes together. That's not friendship, it's killing time."

"Yeah?" I said, letting my anger show in my voice. "Then why . . . "

Vin sighed. "Why did I cut you off, why did I listen to them? I don't know. I was pissed at you for lying, but it wasn't just that. That was my excuse, maybe." He looked straight ahead, tightening his grip on the steering wheel. "The truth is, they think I'm . . . weird for caring as much as I do. I guess it was a relief, not having to care."

I was quiet, afraid of what he was going to say next.

"I told you how messed up I was when you disappeared. Crying in class, all that. Lots of people were like that at first. Including some of them." He shook his head. "Wayne Elementary held this memorial service for you like you were *dead* or something. At eighth-grade graduation they released a white dove in your memory."

"Stop," I said, sickened. "You're making this up."

"No. I wish I was. But see, all that faded. People went on to the next thing. Summer came, and then we started high school, and I was the only one still talking about you. I kind of knew the guys were starting to roll their eyes. But one day Andy came right out and told me to shut up, that I sounded . . . pathetic."

We sat silently for a moment. Then Vin turned to me. "Actually he said I sounded like I was queer for you."

"Oh," I said after a while.

"All I had to do was tell Andy where to shove it. He would have backed down; I know that now. I didn't say anything, though. I let him scare me." Vin hesitated, then spoke in a rush. "I guess I was afraid he could be right. I knew I felt more for you than for anyone else in my life and *that* scared me."

"It's okay," I mumbled, wanting him to stop.

"God, I can see this all now. Andy's always been jealous of you; you're everything he isn't. Even now."

Even now.

"You were my best friend. I should have stood up for you, whether you were there or not. I want us to be friends again, and I don't care what anyone thinks about it."

I shrugged, wanting to detach from him, to end this.

"Jeff, I'm telling you we can go back to school right now and turn this thing around."

"So you're volunteering for the job," I said coldly.

"You want to be my big brother, my protector, my friend. Is that right? Do I have it?"

"Yeah, that's right," Vin said, his eyes challenging me.

"You want to be here for the trial, when Ray trots out all the dirty details?"

"Yeah," Vin nodded. "Whatever, I want to be here for it."

"You don't know what you're talking about. If you did—"

"Jeff, *I don't care.* Okay? Do you get it?"

"I don't believe you," I said flatly. "And it doesn't matter anyway. I'm not coming back to school. So . . ." I caught my breath. "Just forget it, okay?"

"I'm not going to forget it." Vin spoke quietly. "I'm not giving up on you."

My eyes filled with tears. I brushed them back angrily, horrified at myself.

His face stricken, Vin reached over and tapped my shoulder. "Hey, Jeff . . ."

I drew back from him violently, snarling, *"Don't fucking touch me."*

Vin pulled his hand away as if I'd burned it. "I'm sorry," he said. "I didn't mean to —" For the first time, he seemed vulnerable.

"What, are you queer?" I taunted him. "Is that what this is all about? Because if it is . . . " I stopped suddenly, ashamed.

Who's the queer?

Vin regarded me for a long moment, his face reddening.

"This is about me trying to be your friend," he said finally. "When you're ready for that, you let me know."

The ride back to town seemed twice as long as the ride out, and neither of us had anything to say. At my house, I jumped out of the truck, holding the door open so Vin wouldn't roar off like I knew he wanted to.

"Thanks," I said. He stared straight ahead, expressionless. "You know, for what happened in the gym. I'm sorry—"

"No problem. See you around, okay?"

I drew back into myself. "Sure," I said, trailing off, unable to lie to him again. "Goodbye, Vin."

I WAS SPRAWLED ON THE LIVING ROOM COUCH, staring into space, when Charlie and Sherry came in for lunch. Sherry greeted me casually and didn't mention what had happened in the gym.

"I'll be in the kitchen, Charlie," she said, retreating tactfully.

"Okay," Charlie said, her eyes on me. "Jeff, have lunch with us."

I shook my head no, but smiled at her.

"Well . . . you want to play a video game or something later? We could all take turns."

"Nah. I'm fine. Go have your lunch." Charlie nodded, but stayed where she was, hovering at the edge of the room.

"What?" I said, trying to hold on to my patience.

"I talked to Vin," she said abruptly, coming a few steps forward.

I sat up, staring at her. "You talked to him about me?"

After a brief hesitation, she nodded.

Furious with her, I took a deep breath. "Don't

do that, Charlie. Don't talk to him about me. I mean it."

"It wasn't like that," she said, backing up a little. "I just asked if he wanted to come over for lunch today. He said he couldn't."

I nodded, sinking back into the couch.

"But, Jeff! He said he'd like to some other time. He looked really sad, like he—"

"I don't want to talk about this," I warned her. She nodded unhappily.

"Hey," I said, knowing I owed her something. "What you did today took guts." Charlie looked at me. "*You* stood by me, when all that stuff was going on. Not everyone could have done that. Vin couldn't, at first. So . . . thanks."

She smiled slowly, brilliantly, her eyes lighting up. "I liked doing it, Jeff."

"Okay then," I said awkwardly. Charlie came forward and kissed me on the cheek, leaving to join Sherry in the kitchen. I sank back into the couch, thinking about my next hurdle. Dad.

I spent the rest of the afternoon anticipating Dad's arrival, creating and discarding the arguments I would use to convince him I could not go back to school. Charlie returned home around three-thirty, Connie and Brian an hour after that. I barely noticed, cocooned in my room, waiting.

I was too close to Ray and the life he had pressed upon me to fit comfortably into the world of my peers.

The point seemed so obvious now. Why hadn't Dad been able to see it? Worse, why hadn't I fought him on the issue, walking instead into a situation I knew I was not prepared to face?

I knew why, of course. Dad had conspired along with me. *I'm fine*, I had told him so many times, and he had chosen to go along with that, too afraid—too disgusted—to help me face the truth.

Connie announced dinner at six o' clock. I went downstairs only to avoid an explanation of why I could not eat. But she seemed as preoccupied as I was, glancing up at every noise outside, obviously waiting for Dad. When I finally asked what was keeping him, Connie was tight-lipped, saying only that he had been delayed by a problem at work.

By ten o'clock I lay rigid on my bed, furious. *He* was the one pushing school for me, and then he wasn't even around to see how I had done. I should have been relieved, for I still didn't know what I was going to say to him. But as the hours passed, I had only grown more tense. I wanted to tell Dad *now*, have the argument *now*, that I would not be returning to school.

I turned on my side, under the covers, dressed for bed in a T-shirt and sweatpants, miles away from sleep. Ray spoke to me—

Love you.

And Vin—

You were makin' it with that guy.

And the voices from school—

Fag.

You miss getting it regular?

I flipped over again, angry with myself, reaching up to snap the light on. Maybe I could borrow a book from Charlie . . .

"How did everything go today?" Dad asked quietly, standing in the hallway just outside my bedroom.

I was speechless, choked with anger and shame. He came a few steps into the room, looking as though he already knew the answer.

"Not so good," I said. Dad nodded. "I . . . I don't think I want to go back. I'm sorry." I waited tensely for his questions, for the lecture he would be sure to give me on perseverance.

Dad nodded again, running a hand through his hair. "I've had some second thoughts myself about you going back to that school. It's tough here, where everyone knows you. We'll talk it over tomorrow, all right?"

"There's nothing to talk over," I said, relieved and disappointed, trying to bait him into a reaction.

Come on, Dad, care. Tell me not to give up.

"Well," he said, "not tonight, anyway. I'll see you tomorrow."

Dad walked out of my room looking defeated. I hated him. I hated myself.

THE MAN I CAME TO KNOW AS "RAY" HELD THE *knife against my neck as he pushed my face down into the dark blue carpeting of the van. Kneeling on the backs of my thighs, he pulled one of my arms back, then the other, and cuffed my hands together. I raised my head to scream but before I could open my mouth, the man dove forward and threw his full weight on top of me. I felt the knife against my cheek and the man's breath on my hair as he ordered me to open my mouth wide. His hand shook as he held the blade close to my eye and I began to cry as I opened my mouth for him. Placing his knife on the carpet, so close to my head the blade touched my nose, he pushed a soft, wadded cloth into my mouth, securing it with a knotted rag he fastened tightly around my head.*

The man sat back on my body, resting on my thighs again, breathing heavily. I fought for air as mucus filled my throat and tears ran across my face down into my nose. I closed my eyes to try to hold back the tears, relaxing into the man's rhythm for a moment.

He must have felt the tension leave my body, for he reared back off of my thighs. Instantly my body told me to kick back at him, to use my legs against him while I still could. But I was too close to the memory of suffocating. The knife lay in front of me, so close I could smell the hot metal of the blade. What would he do if I kicked at him and missed? Or struck a blow that hurt him without knocking him out? I remained passive, and he pushed my legs together, binding them tightly with something that felt like a long belt.

The man crawled over me, pausing to pick up his knife, and climbed into the driver's seat. He took a deep breath, then started the van.

He continued north for a while, and I allowed myself some hope. Someone at the rest stop must have seen the van and would connect it with my disappearance: it would not be hard for my family to find me.

I lay flat, my head bent sharply to one side, the rough carpet scratching against my cheek. My arms and legs were beginning to fall asleep. In the front of the van, the man was silent.

Suddenly he changed lanes, so quickly the momentum rolled me off my stomach. The handcuffs dug sharply into my back and I tried to cry out, raising my body off my arms, falling back down on them again.

Another shift and I knew he was leaving the highway. My stomach turned over as he drove a short distance, stopped, turned left, then left again, accelerating. We were heading south now, down Highway 99 in the opposite direction, and I thought maybe he had had a change of heart, that he was taking me back to the rest stop. But he kept driving, until I knew we had to be far beyond that point. I cried silently, keeping my eyes tightly shut to stop the tears from choking me.

I became used to the feel of the handcuffs digging into my back. It was only when the van's motion threw me off them, and the continuous pressure was relieved, that I was aware of the pain. I would have a bruise there, I knew, a good one. I felt the chafing of my wrists too as the skin wore away, and I pictured the marks the cuffs would leave.

"Maybe he'll never take them off," I realized. "Maybe whatever he wants me for, he doesn't need to take them off. Maybe they'll find me like this."

The tears came again, but this time I blinked them back.

"Stop feeling sorry for yourself," I thought. "Fight, figure it out, do something."

From the position I was in I could see out the top part of the front passenger-side window. We passed tall buildings, and billboards, and silos. At one point we drove alongside a semi-truck and I saw the profile of the driver inside.

"If I can see him," I thought, "maybe he can see me." Hope flared, then died as many more miles went by without sirens, without the man noticeably changing his speed. I watched the sky begin to darken.

I had to go to the bathroom bad. There was no way

to ask. I wouldn't go in my pants. I had that much pride.

The man shifted again, quickly, changing lanes, then exiting the freeway. I rolled, landing on my stomach, and my arms and legs began to tingle, then burn, as the circulation began to return. I had to cough, too, but I couldn't with the gag, and I began to hack in the back of my throat. The man swore and sped up.

I couldn't breathe through my mouth, and I couldn't take in enough air through my nose, which was still congested from the crying I had done. I began to choke, my chest heaving. I was going to die. I could feel it.

He pulled off sharply onto another road, tires squealing, then, almost immediately, made another quick turn. The van screeched to a stop and the man jumped out the driver's-side door. I heard him running around the van to the back panel doors. He swore again as he fumbled with the lock, then threw the doors open and pulled me out by my feet.

I crashed to the ground, my head narrowly missing the back bumper. The man knelt beside me. Taking his knife, he cut through the rag around my head, then pulled the cloth out of my mouth. I heaved, trying to catch my breath. My mouth was bone-dry, and I could taste fibers from the cloth all through it. I rolled to my side, coughing weakly, my head rubbing against the hard-packed dirt.

"Now," he said, sounding worried, "I am going to

let your arms and legs loose and you go ahead and cough. If you do anything else, or try to run, I'll hurt you. Understand?"

I nodded. Reaching into his back pocket, he unlocked the cuffs, then took the knife and cut through the belt that bound my legs. Sharp pains shot through my limbs and I cried out, but the need to cough was greater. Raising myself to my hands and knees, I coughed deep from the gut. The man rubbed my back and made soothing noises. A persistent tickle in my throat maddened me to the point that I couldn't concentrate on anything else.

"Water, please," I choked out.

He leaned forward. "What?"

With all the strength I had left I sat up a little. "Water," I said slowly. "Please." Another coughing fit hit me and I doubled over.

"Oh, sure. Water," he said, making no move to get any. "How do I know you won't run? It's in the front seat of the van."

"I won't," I gasped.

"I'll get you if you do," he warned.

He moved away from me, and I heard him rustling around in the front of the van. The pressure on my bladder was unbearable. For the first time in my memory, I peed my pants, flooding my shorts, the hot urine burning against my legs. He came back with the water as I finished, my eyes closed in shame.

The man said nothing, kneeling by me again and

helping me sit up. He held my head back and poured water into my mouth clumsily, spilling it all over my jersey. I drank gratefully, reaching up to hold the jug to my mouth.

"That's enough," he said, pulling the jug away from me and setting it just inside the back of the van. "You okay now?"

I dared to look at him. The man had dark hair, pale skin, a mustache and an unshaven face. His eyes were black and unblinking and he took my face in as if he was memorizing it.

"I asked if you were okay," he said harshly.

"I think so," I told him. He pulled the handcuffs out of his back pocket and took hold of one of my wrists. I pulled back and he yanked me forward twice as hard. "No, please," I said, dignity forgotten in the memory of the pain, the feeling of being trapped. "You don't need to handcuff me."

The man half smiled, half sneered. "Why not?"

"I won't try to get away," I said quickly. "I won't run. You don't have to tie me up." The sky was overcast, the moon half-hidden behind a cloud. Distant mountains ringed the flat land where we knelt, and the air was heavy with the smell of fertilizer. I heard the sounds of the freeway not far off, but I could see no lights from cars or any other human source. The man and I were utterly alone.

"You'd be stupid to run," he said, smiling a little. "You wouldn't last long out here without me." The

man nodded to himself, looking down. His lip curled. "You wet yourself, didn't you?"

The two of us were kneeling in a puddle of my urine. I could smell it suddenly, hot and sharp.

"I'm . . . sorry," I said, feeling dizzy. "I had to, I couldn't . . . "

"It's okay," he said matter-of-factly, "but this is a new van. I want to keep it clean. Let's get these clothes off you."

My stomach dipped and I began to shiver. "No, that's okay, it'll dry fast. It's a warm night, so . . . "

"Come on," he said, standing up and pulling me with him, "let's get 'em off."

"Look," I said desperately, "please don't do this. I won't tell anyone anything if you just leave me here. I don't know you, I don't know where I am, they'll never find you, so . . . please just leave me here."

The man smiled slowly at me. "Relax. You pissed your pants, and I want to clean you up."

Maybe he's just crazy, I told myself. Shivering, I stood still as he reached for the buttons on my shorts. I tried to ignore the way his hands lingered on my hips as he eased my shorts and underwear down.

"Step out of them," he ordered. "Now your shoes and socks."

I knelt to untie my shoes, taking my time about it, afraid to face him again. He kicked my hand lightly and, shocked, I almost fell, the cold metal of the van's bumper hard against my back.

"Stand up," the man said, his voice husky now. I averted my eyes, but I couldn't help noticing the bulge in his jeans. "Now pull off that jersey."

Still looking away from him, I obeyed, bundling the jersey up in my hand.

He reached into the van for the jug of water, then splashed it across my lower torso.

"Dry yourself," he ordered. "Use the jersey."

I complied, rubbing the sweaty material over my body and legs.

He reached into the van again, pulling out a green garbage bag and handing it to me. "Put your stuff in this. All of it. Shoes, shorts, everything."

Trembling uncontrollably, I did as he asked.

"You got pee all over my jeans too," the man said. Smiling, he reached down and unbuttoned himself.

I leaned against the wall outside Dad and Connie's bedroom, waiting for the fear to subside. It was no good this time. My heart pounded against my chest with an intensity that scared me, and all I could hear was the sound of my own ragged breath.

Light flooded the hallway. I stepped away from the wall, drawing in my breath, my heartbeat crescendoing in my ears.

"Jeff!" Dad was saying. "What is it, what's wrong?"

I turned around slowly, focusing in on him. Dad still wore his suit, minus the jacket. He had come up the stairs behind me. He hadn't been in the room at all.

I shook my head, still scared, and angry too. "Where were you?" I said, my voice cracking.

"Where was I?" Dad repeated softly. "What . . . I was downstairs, Jeff. I'm doing some work at home—"

"No!" I interrupted him. "Not now. Before!"

He watched me carefully, tilting his head. "Come downstairs. Let's talk about it."

"No," I said, weaker this time. Dad waited, his face

calm. I heard Connie beginning to stir and that gave me the excuse I needed to follow him.

Dad's office was the only room lit downstairs. I expected him to lead me there, but he walked past it, continuing on into the living room. I paused at the office door, glancing inside. Dad's desk was strewn with loose papers anchored down by a heavy law book. The book was open, a yellow legal pad on top of it, an uncapped pen resting on top of that. For some reason I could not name, the arrangement filled me with dread.

Dad waited for me in the living room, already seated. I mumbled an apology he ignored, motioning me to the couch opposite. I sat down carefully, noticing how tired he looked. I shook off my instinctive sympathy, knowing that I must be the cause of whatever tired him so.

"What are you thinking about right now?" Dad said, peering at me suddenly. I gaped at him, then shook my head.

"What was going on upstairs then?"

"Nothing," I said automatically. Then, like that, I told him the truth.

"Sometimes when I can't sleep, I stand outside your room. Doing that usually makes me feel safer." I looked down, my face burning.

Dad went right past that. "Why couldn't you sleep? Why tonight, in particular? Something must have happened at school."

"It wasn't that. At least . . . that wasn't the only reason."

Dad nodded, waiting.

"I was remembering stuff. Usually I can push it away. Tonight I couldn't."

"What stuff? Can you tell me? Please."

My courage deserted me. "No. Sorry."

Dad sighed, looking down at his hands, then at me. "Okay. What happened at school today? Why don't you want to go back?"

I shrugged, half angry he had not pushed me more. "Nothing that different from what I thought would happen. I just didn't know how bad it would feel."

"Kids gave you a hard time." It was not a question.

"Yeah. And I'm not going back. I don't care what you say. I'm not ready for them, and they're sure not ready for me."

"Jeff . . . "

I held up a hand to stop him. "Don't tell me to 'hang tough' or anything like that. I'm not going back. They act like I did something wrong, that I *am* wrong. It's not fair."

"No," he agreed softly, clasping his hands together and staring at them. I had expected a fight from him, and my adrenaline was up to fight him back. *Don't give up on me, Dad. Don't agree with me that I'm hopeless.*

"Vin too, I suppose?"

"He was with them at first, with the worst of them. Then he switched sides. Now he says he wants to help me."

"That's not so bad," Dad said carefully. "He's a kid. Like you."

"Not like me," I mumbled. "No one's like me." A shudder ran through me as I realized how alone I was. Trapped in my own head with Ray, and no way out.

"Jeff," Dad called sharply, not for the first time, I realized. "What I've been doing with you isn't working. I've backed off, I've tried to let you handle this your way. But it's not working."

I watched him fearfully. "What do you want me to do?"

"I want you to tell me about Slaight. I want you to tell me what he did to you. You're making yourself sick holding this stuff in. If you never testify against him, Dave won't be happy, but I can live with that. I want you to talk to me."

Mingled with my horror and embarrassment, I felt something like hope.

"You say that, Dad, but you don't really want to know."

"I do."

"You don't want to know—you can't—what it was like, living with him every day."

"Jeff," Dad said, "please tell me. I'm ready to listen."

Confused, I looked away from him, shaking my head.

"All right." Dad's voice was calm, his tone measured. "So you never talk about Slaight. You live with it by yourself. You don't go to school—"

"Fuck school!"

He nodded. "Okay. Fuck school. We'll just keep tiptoeing around you, pretending nothing is wrong. Hell, we might as well invite Slaight to move in with us. He's here anyway."

"Don't say that." I was trembling. "Don't ever say that." Dad did not apologize, just watched me, no expression on his face.

"You want to know why I came back so thin?" I said suddenly.

"Yes."

"He hardly fed me. Ray. He would just laugh when I asked him. I had to beg him for food."

Dad watched me steadily, unblinking.

"Sometimes I had to do stuff for him—sexual stuff—if I wanted to eat."

"All right," Dad said, after a moment.

"All right," I repeated, laughing in disbelief.

"What would you like me to say?"

"Say the truth! Tell me I'm disgusting."

Dad looked down. When he looked at me again, his eyes were moist. "I'm not disgusted, Jeff."

"He taught me to . . . " Even now, I could not tell Dad the specifics. "He taught me to have sex with him the way he wanted it. That's what I learned, Dad. That was my education."

A beat. Then Dad nodded. "Yes."

I glared at him. "Do you even hear what I'm saying?"

"Yes. I hear what you're saying."

"I gave in to him. I did what he wanted. Not once. Hundreds of times."

"You had no choice," Dad said fiercely. I stared at him, surprised by the sudden emotion in his voice. "No choice at all."

I waited a long moment. Then I shrugged, watching him. "Upstairs, you know. Before. I was remembering the first time with Ray. The first time he had sex with me."

Dad nodded. "I'd like you to tell me about that."

"*What?*" I laughed in anger and disbelief. He had no right. "Oh, Dad, come on."

"You lived through it," he said. "I should be able to hear about it."

Suddenly I was furious with him. "It's not that easy. You think listening to me talk about this shit *changes* any of it? It doesn't. It won't."

"I know that. But don't you see, if I know everything you went through, I can help you more, and together we can—"

"Where were you?" I asked, more to stop his words than anything else.

Dad froze. "Where was I when?" He knew.

I closed my eyes as I said the words I had so often thought. "Where were you when I was in that room? Where were you when I was alone with him? I waited for you. I counted on you. You never came."

When I could not stand the silence any longer, I looked at him. Dad's head was lowered, his fists clenched on his thighs. My instinct was to comfort him, to retreat. I ignored the impulse, watching him calmly. Finally he looked up.

"I tried to find you. I tried every way I knew how. I stayed in Fresno for weeks after you disappeared, searching for you personally. I made the rounds of the law enforcement agencies every day. I screamed until they brought the FBI in.

"We contacted schools across the country," Dad continued, talking fast. "Twice a year, every semester, right up until last fall. Connie typed the letters, I made the calls, the kids stuffed envelopes. . . . "

"You thought I was going to school somewhere?" I bit back the urge to laugh.

Dad looked at me sharply. "I had no idea where you were. *I didn't know.* That was the hell of it. I never knew if I was an inch away from finding you, or if I was running like hell in the opposite direction."

He was grim-faced after that, silent for so long I felt I had to say something. "I'm sorry. . . . "

"Don't be sorry. Just listen. After you had been gone a few months, the FBI lost interest. Dave never gave up, and I'll always be grateful to him for that, but he was one person, and yours wasn't the only case he was working. I set up a toll-free number for people to call with tips about you, and I followed up on them myself. I traveled to Houston, Kansas City, New Orleans, New York, Los Angeles three times looking for you. I'd plaster the town with posters, appear on whatever media would have me, haunt the police stations . . . anything I could think of to get the word out."

"Dad . . . "

"I visited coroners' offices, Jeff," he said deliberately. "All across the country. About every six months I'd get the call, they'd found some body, some poor kid who half-resembled you. I went every time. Not because I believed any of those boys could be you. But I knew if I didn't see them with my own eyes, I wouldn't have been able to live with myself."

I squirmed, uncomfortable. "Okay, Dad."

"I hired a private detective out of L.A. He heard a rumor you might be involved in kiddy porn and he started sending me boxes of the stuff to scour for pictures of you." I looked at him quickly, and he nodded. "Oh yes, I did that too, until Brian got into it one day when I wasn't home and Connie got hysterical. So we stopped that and then I tortured myself with the idea that maybe you would have been in the next magazine—"

"Dad, you made your point."

"For the better part of two years," he said, talking over me, "I did almost nothing else but try to find you. I came damn close to bankruptcy, to losing this house, my job—everything we still had. The only reason I pulled out of it, actually, was to preserve the family for you. I knew you would come home one day, and when you did, you would need that structure."

I sat dumbly on the couch, staring down at my hands.

"I'm not looking for your sympathy. I know none of that was enough. I didn't find you, and that's the bottom line. You had to save yourself."

I looked up at him, wondering if I'd heard correctly. "What?"

"I couldn't do it for you," Dad said, "so you saved yourself."

The idea was so radical I could only stare at him. "*Save* myself? What . . . I didn't save myself. I'm screwed up, Dad. Screwed up and screwed over," I added deliberately.

He didn't flinch. "You're alive. You convinced Slaight to bring you home. You won."

"You know how I convinced him, don't you? You've known it all along." I looked away. "I don't see how you can know that and not hate me for it, even a little."

"Jeff." He waited until I met his eyes. "The things Slaight did to you, the fact that he used you sexually"— Dad hit the words hard—"I hate him for it, of course. Not you. Never you."

"But I was there too, Dad." I took a deep breath. "Anyway, it wasn't just the sex. Ray . . . loved me, I think. He told me so and I built on that. He was kinder to me then, so I . . . that's how I fought him. I convinced Ray that I loved him. I kissed him back, Dad. Do you get it? *I kissed him back.*"

"I get it," Dad said roughly. "And I'm telling you, good. If that worked, good."

"You don't know the details. You don't know how I was with him. You don't know everything I did."

Dad shook his head slightly. "There is nothing you

can tell me, nothing I can find out, that will ever make me turn away from you."

"Is that true?" I asked after a moment.

"Yes," he said simply.

I closed my eyes, trying to absorb what he was offering: unconditional love. Unconditional acceptance. I felt lighter, the pressure I had come to accept as normal lifting away from my chest. I took a deep breath, letting it out as a memory hit me like a fist in the stomach.

"When I told you about my back, you stopped touching me."

"Yes," Dad said. My stomach turned over. I hadn't expected him to agree with me. "I thought that was what you wanted."

I stared at him. He was right. Yet . . . "Dad, it wasn't just that you didn't touch me anymore. You could barely stand to look at me after that."

Dad lowered his head. "Spare a thought for me in all this. How do you think I felt when you told me about your back? I wanted to kill Slaight, but I knew whatever I did to him wouldn't help you now. I felt so guilty, so . . . helpless, I had a hard time facing myself, much less you."

I had to know for sure. "You didn't stop touching me because . . . because you thought I was disgusting?"

He shook his head slowly. "No" was all he said. It was all he needed to say.

We sat quietly for a moment.

"He scarred you," Dad said. I gasped, sitting back in

the chair. "Not just physically. I know he's living in your head now. Maybe you feel he's still with you . . . "

"He is."

"You can heal, Jeff," Dad said intensely. "You will."

"Scars don't heal," I told him with a short laugh. "That's why they're scars."

"Tell me what you see when you look at your back," Dad said.

"I don't look."

"Then what do you imagine?"

"Cords," I said immediately. "That's what they feel like. The scars. Sometimes I think of them as worms. Thick white worms gliding across my back . . . " Tears slipped down my cheeks. I stopped talking before my voice veered out of control.

"Let me see."

I waited for a feeling of outrage, or panic, to give me the energy I needed to turn Dad down, turn him down in such language he would never ask me again.

It didn't come. Instead I felt tired, and weak, only a small spark of fear making me hesitate. Who cared anymore?

I stood up slowly, moving over to where he sat. I turned around, pulling my T-shirt halfway up, keeping it in place with my arms tight by my sides.

Dad stood behind me, pressing one hand lightly against my neck to move me forward. I took two steps and listened to his breathing.

"It's not so bad, Jeff," he said after a while, his voice thick. "May I touch your back?"

"Okay," I said, working to keep my voice casual. I felt like running when I felt Dad's cool fingers on me, but I stayed where I was.

He pushed his hand up under my shirt, rubbing my upper back gently. I shivered suddenly as gooseflesh covered my arms. Dad worked his way down, his hand moving from one side of my back to the other, his fingers now barely grazing the skin. Each mark tingled as he hit it, until I imagined the stripes illuminating, one after the other, on the canvas of my back.

Dad took his hand away and, so gently it brought fresh tears to my eyes, pushed my arms up from my sides and pulled the T-shirt back down around me. I kept my eyes down as he turned me around to face him.

"I want you to look, too," he said quietly. "I want you to see what I saw." He sounded tense, waiting for my protest.

"Okay," I said. I trailed after him to the guest bedroom, to the full-length mirror on the outside of the closet door. I stood in front of the mirror, staring at my feet, while Dad went into the bathroom.

He returned with a hand mirror, which he gave to me. "I'm going to wait in the living room. You look as much as you need to, and then come back and join me."

"Okay, Dad," I said, feeling fragile.

He left, closing the door behind him.

He trusts me.

I took my shirt off, tossing it on the bed, then turned around slowly, my back to the mirror. I held the hand mirror to the right of my face, peering into it.

I saw nothing more than my back gleaming whitely, and I looked away quickly, feeling hope and anger mixed. I knew what I had seen could not be the truth.

Moving to the lamp by the guest bed, I flicked it on to add more light to the room. I returned to the closet mirror, closer this time. Taking a deep breath, I held the hand mirror up again, angling downward to get a better look.

It was then I saw what I had felt for so long: my back scored by a fine tracing of white lines that extended from below my neck to just above my buttocks. The scars were faint, but visible. Two of them, on my lower back, stood up slightly from the skin.

My fear, which in some corner of myself I had known to be untrue, was that my back was a patchwork of hideous, disfiguring ridges. I could see that was not the case. But my fantasy, which I had been able to hold until this moment, was that nothing was visible, that my back was as smooth and innocent as the day I had been kidnapped. That wasn't true either.

Dad leaned back against the couch, his eyes shut, arms stretched out across the top. I stood in the doorway, watching him.

"Dad," I said softly when it became apparent he didn't know I was there.

He sat up quickly, rubbing his eyes. "What do you think?"

I shrugged. "Not so bad, I guess."

"That's what I was thinking," he said carefully. "Not so bad at all."

"Not so good, either," I added.

Dad waited a moment, then nodded. "Come sit beside me," he urged, patting a spot on the couch next to him. I picked my way over, sitting farther down the couch than where he'd indicated.

"I'll never be normal again," I said after a while, needing to hear his reassurance, knowing I could not believe it.

"I don't know what that word means. You're here and I love you. That's all I care about."

"He's lying," I said abruptly. Dad looked over at me. "Ray. Those things he said about me. I wasn't hitch-hiking. I didn't ask to stay with him."

"Oh, Jeff," Dad started, sounding angry. I tensed. "Of course he's lying," he said more calmly. "Of course he is. Everyone will know that. That's not something you have to worry about."

"The kids at school believe him," I said.

"Do they?" Dad asked gently. "All of them?"

"Maybe not," I said. "Dad, why did this have to happen to me?"

He sighed deeply, closing his eyes. "I don't know."

"He raped me," I said, testing the words to see how it felt to say them out loud. "He *raped* me," I said again, feeling the shell of my detachment falling away. "How could he do that to me? How could he treat me that way?"

"I don't know," Dad murmured.

"I hate him so much. *I hate him*," I screamed.

Dad was crying. "I hate him too," he said, holding

his arms out to me. I hesitated only a moment. Dad pulled me to him, half onto his lap.

Ray Ray Ray

"No," I shouted, holding Dad tighter. As if he understood, he wrapped his arms around me, holding me close to his chest, kissing my cheek.

If Ray saw us now, he'd laugh and he'd say . . .

"I hate him, Dad," I said again, my voice muffled.

"I know, baby, I know."

"Don't call me that," I moaned. He stopped stroking my hair for a moment, and I felt his sudden intake of breath.

"Slaight doesn't own words," Dad said finally. "Most of all, he doesn't own you. He's nothing to do with you now."

I nodded, listening to his heartbeat, knowing I looked ridiculous, more six than sixteen, feeling safer than I had since I'd come home. Dad kissed the top of my head, murmuring endearments as if I were a little child. Gradually I let myself relax into his embrace.

We stayed that way for a long time, so long I felt myself falling asleep against his chest. I didn't want that—the idea panicked me—and I tried to sit up.

"Dad," I said awkwardly, a little scared, "I'm pretty tired. Maybe I should go up to my room now." He released me at once and I pushed myself off his lap. I sat next to him, embarrassed, facing the other way.

"Hey," Dad said questioningly. I felt his light touch on the back of my head.

Without answering him or looking back, I nodded. I didn't pull away from the pressure of his hand.

"Why don't you sleep here?" Dad said. He cleared his throat. I turned around to look at him. "I'll stay here and you can rest your head on my lap—if you want."

I knew he needed the physical contact with me, needed it as much as I did.

My head on his lap? I couldn't, that was sick, that's like something Ray . . .

"Okay," I said.

Dad nodded. "Good," he said. I stretched out full-length, and laid my head on his thigh, feeling the warmth of his flannelled leg. After a moment Dad began to stroke my hair.

Something had been nagging at me, something outside myself.

"Why were you so late tonight?" I asked sleepily. He stopped what he was doing, his hand motionless upon my head.

"Slaight's about to make bail. I'm doing everything I can to stop him."

"But you think he will."

Dad hesitated. "I . . . yes, I think he might." I didn't respond, and he went back to touching my hair.

"You need another haircut," he said, almost to himself.

I smiled faintly. "Could Mel cut it?" I asked, trying to sound casual. "Maybe I could go to San Francisco with you tomorrow. Meet with Stephens or something, if you want to arrange it."

Dad waited, resting his fingers lightly on my skull. "Is that what you want to do, Jeff?"

I turned onto my back and looked up at him. My father.

He watched me, ready, I knew, to accept anything I told him.

"Yeah," I said, "I think I'm ready to talk."